DEA

T.R.Schumer is a writer and ad

who once copiloted a single-engine aircraft around the world, an
avid scuba diver, and sailor. The author is currently sailing around
the world, and as of 2016, after departing from Palma de Majorca
in the Balearic Islands, has reached the halfway mark of New Zealand.

DEATH CATCH

Book 1 of the *Fearless* Trilogy

T R Schumer

Death Catch, Book 1 of the *Fearless* Trilogy
Copyright © 2016 by T. R. Schumer
All Rights Reserved Worldwide

Published by T. R. Schumer
ISBN-13: 978-976-95924-1-4
Printed Edition v1 - April 2016

Cover Design by Damonza
Editing by Scribendi

Honey, we're a team...

Prologue

West Africa, in the year 1247...

The impala's head quickly rises above a thick hedge of parched savannah grass. Ever vigilant, ever wary, it watches for predators as it nervously chews. One of a herd of twenty, the animal's sleek bronze and white coat shines under the morning sun while its brushy tail rapidly chases away flies. It diligently scans the shimmering, sun-soaked horizon, but the yearling buck's large eyes see nothing. His wide ears flip forward, then back, but no sound signals danger. The buck drops his head once more, reaching down to crop off another mouthful of grass just as the spear point enters his left side.

The finely sharpened iron blade passes cleanly between the impala's third and fourth ribs. Velocity drives the spear point through the left lung, its inertia terminating only after the spear's long lethal tip severs the impala's pulmonary artery, releasing the life from its body before the animal even realizes it has been killed. The impact triggers a panic response; the impala leaps high into

1

the air while the long slender spear handle jutting from the buck's side flies about in an odd circle. The impala hits the ground and launches into a dead run; the buck manages three long strides before he drops to the ground.

Two young boys emerge from the grass. Elike is twelve years old; his little brother Mawuko is nine. As they locate the trail of blood left behind by their prey, the younger boy congratulates his older sibling.

"Father will be proud," Mawuko says admiringly.

"No," answers Elike. "But mother will be happy."

"Of course Father will be proud. You are a great hunter!"

"No, I won't be a great hunter until I have killed a buffalo, or a leopard," the older boy replies.

Mawuko eagerly keeps pace with his older brother as the pair track the bright red blood trail lying wet and glistening across the dry grass. They quickly find the impala, and Mawuko smiles. "You are a great hunter."

The impala's body trembles with rapid shallow breaths as it struggles to hold on to the last moments of its life; the spear handle now stands nearly straight up from the impala's side. The two boys approach confidently. "The animal must be killed quickly," Elike instructs. Grabbing the spear's slender wood shaft with both hands, he rapidly twists it, and then jerks it from the animal's body. "You see? Just like that, it is done. Now we must pray for the animal's spirit; we must thank him for feeding our village."

Their prize, field dressed, now hangs upside down from a wooden walking stick stretched between their shoulders as the two boys trek back to their home. The midday sun beats down on the boys as they walk. "We should rest," Elike announces. They veer off the path and head for the shade of a nearby tree. Soon after he sits, Mawuko begins to play with some small stones he has found on the ground.

"Why do you do this?" his older brother chides. "Soon you will be a man like me. Only children play as you do."

"Aiee!" Mawuko cries as he quickly draws his hand back from the dirt.

"What have you done? Is it a snake? A scorpion?" Elike grabs the boy's hand. "What is it this time?" He examines Mawuko's hand carefully as the boy sobs. "I see nothing. What are you crying about?" Mawuko points down at the small stones he had been playing with. His older brother picks up a twig and begins pushing the stones around when a brief bright glimmer catches the sunlight. "What is this?" Elike pokes at the stones some more, and uncovers the shining object. He's never seen anything like it. A stone of sorts, but remarkably smooth and lustrous. Reaching for his leather hunting pouch, Elike pulls out a piece of cloth. Using it to carefully pick up the object, he holds it out into the light as it flashes, dazzling his eyes. He examines it closely, then Elike wraps it up inside the cloth, and places it inside his pouch.

As the two young hunters arrive home, the boys are greeted warmly by their mother and two older sisters, while their father inspects the impala. "It was a clean kill, Father," Elike reports, but his father says nothing; his face shows no expression as he examines the carcass. He tells the two girls to carry the animal inside, a gesture that signals his approval. As the girls quickly take the impala from their brothers' shoulders, Elike approaches his father. "Father, I have something for you." He pulls the cloth from his pouch, then opens it to reveal the shining, highly polished piece of glimmering, hardened metal. Its slender oval shape and clean edges are so precisely fashioned, the boy's father is stunned at the sight of it.

Although he tries hard not to react, Elike's father's eyes grow large. "This is an important gift you have found, my son. It is a sign."

The boy carefully lays the cloth in his father's outstretched hands. "Be careful, Father," Elike warns, "it bites."

The man hesitates momentarily, then draws his hands in close as he stares intensely at the small object's sparkling, impossibly smooth surface. He then carefully wraps the cloth back around it. He looks at his oldest son, and speaks to him in a voice that is almost a whisper, "Go help your mother."

Elike's father decides to walk to the home of the village shaman. If anyone knows the meaning of this object, it will be him. As he approaches, the shaman emerges from his house.

"So," the shaman begins, "it was Elike and Mawuko who carried the impala into the village today?"

"Yes." The man is surprised. "How did you know?"

"It was in my vision," the shaman answers. "You have brought me something?"

"I have," the man says. He opens the cloth and shows the magical object to the shaman. The shaman's expression doesn't change as he carefully examines it.

"Yes, I saw this object in my vision, it holds great power; a remarkable gift... perhaps the spirits have been kind to us." The shaman then looks into his chief's eyes. "You must bring me the bones of the impala. They must be perfectly clean."

Two days later, the chief's daughters arrive at the shaman's home bearing the meticulously cleaned bones of the impala clustered inside a large basket. The shaman takes the basket from the two sisters, places it on the ground, and opens it. He politely thanks them for cleaning the bones so beautifully, then sends the girls on their way. Lifting the basket, the shaman disappears into his mud brick and thatched home. Once inside, he turns the basket upside down and allows the bones to spill out onto a woven grass mat. He examines the pattern carefully, prays, then makes his selection; the right front cannon bone. He ties a leather string to the bone he has chosen, then the shaman hangs it from a support beam, and carefully buries the rest.

One month later the shaman takes down the fully dried leg bone of the impala. He hollows out the bone's interior and begins to carve a small statue representing the spirit of the animal. He spends a number of days carefully fashioning the small talisman. Once completed to his satisfaction, the shaman carefully places the object inside the statue. He secures it in place with beeswax, then seals the open ends of the statue with more carved bone. Once completed, the statue looks as if it were carved from a solid piece of bone; no seams are visible, the workmanship is intricate, its surface expertly finished.

Over the course of the following year, word spread and stories began to be told of the remarkable healing power the shaman possessed. Infected wounds that should have been fatal, an outbreak of fever sickness, and even a cobra bite were all healed. People began to travel from neighboring villages to visit the shaman, and under the chief's direction, he healed them all.

Then one day, a group of warriors from a rival village carry a dying young man to the doorstep of the shaman's home. They tell the shaman how they were hunting when a lion attacked. They killed the lion, but not before it ravaged the youngest of their hunting party, the son of the rival chief. The shaman has the young man brought inside, where the warriors lay him out on the same grass mat the shaman had spread the impala's bones on the year before, and immediately he goes to work.

After three days of waiting outside the house of the shaman, the warriors are shocked to see the young man emerge from the shaman's home. Walking under his own power, he tells them of his incredible healing journey to the spirit world and back. To celebrate this miracle, the chief holds a feast in the young man's honor, with the rival chief's son taking his seat beside Elike and Mawuko. During the celebration, the chief makes a moving speech out of respect for his guests. In it he thanks the spirits for giving him the opportunity to bring the two rival villages together. He expresses his gratitude to the young warriors for bringing the chief's wounded son to the shaman so that he may be healed, and with him, heal the years of rivalry between their people.

The next day the warriors depart for their home, but not before the son of the rival chief makes a promise that he and his fellow warriors will tell his father how he survived, and that the two villages must now make peace.

On the warrior's journey home, however, the young men grow increasingly fearful as the chief's son begins to change his attitude. He starts to speak incessantly of his newfound power, as he talks about the day when his father will die, and he will be chief. He begins to speak of himself as a god, as a man who cannot be killed. Then, on the fourth day of their journey, the chief's son announces that he has changed his mind about peace, that once he gains power, he plans to seize all of the neighboring villages under his rule, a rule that will last forever.

That night, as the chief's son sleeps, the warriors talk quietly amongst themselves. They fear he has gone insane, and that the shaman's magic somehow caused it. They agree the chief's son is too dangerous. "He has been possessed by dark spirits; we must stop him now," the oldest of their party proclaims. They cast a vote to decide the fate of the chief's son, and once the vote is cast, the warriors take up their knives and kill him. They carry his body back to their home village, and lay it at the feet of his father as his mother wails with grief. They tell their chief that they saw the shaman use black magic, and when they tried to stop him, they were ambushed by warriors from the rival village who killed his son.

• • •

Raising his spear, Elike checks that the base of the shaft is mounted securely in the cup of his throwing stick. He then takes careful aim as the leopard he has been tracking for the past three days sharpens its claws on a nearby tree. Elike lets loose a powerful throw, but the spear point only strikes the leopard in the shoulder. The big cat is wounded, but not mortally. As Elike raises up from the grass to face the wounded cat, Mawuko calls to him, "No, brother, let me help you! Let me throw my spear!"

"No, Mawuko," his older brother commands, "stay where you are. I must kill him myself." The leopard growls and hisses while a trickle of blood runs down the shaft of the spear hanging from its shoulder. Elike approaches confidently. The boy has his knife out; he is ready. Elike studies the big cat carefully as he waits for the leopard to make his move. The young hunter is only three meters away when the leopard lunges at him. Elike is quick; in one continuous motion he smoothly avoids the leopard's claws, then jams his knife into the cat's throat. As the two of them fall to the ground, Elike stabs the cat once more in the lung. As the two boys stand over the body of the leopard, Mawuko is smiling. "Now brother, now you are truly a great hunter."

"Perhaps," Elike answers, "but now that I have killed him, I also mourn for him."

An excited, noisy crowd of children gather eagerly around Elike and Mawuko as the brothers enter their village carrying the magnificent leopard. As they approach their home, their father the chief is waiting. He looks Elike in the eye as his son presents him with the leopard, and for a brief instant, Elike sees him smile. Then suddenly, more shouting is heard, but it's not the children, it's a group of returning herdsmen. They have come to warn the chief of an impending attack. "How can this be?" the chief asks in disbelief. "We made peace. How can they be attacking us?"

One of the herdsmen steps forward. "We were told by a hunting party that the chief's son died on the way home. The hunters told us they saw the warriors pass by, they saw the chief's son walking amongst them, but later they learned that he had been killed by knifepoint. In their fear, the warriors have blamed the shaman's magic for his death, but it is they themselves who are responsible; for what reason? Only the gods know. Now their chief has launched an attack on us; he has gathered his allies. They say we practice black magic, and that our village is a source of evil. We came to warn you as soon as we could."

* * *

The next day, in another village, where the shaman has been working to cure an outbreak of fever sickness, he receives word that his own village has been massacred. Devastated by the news, the shaman leaves immediately. For two days the shaman walks in silence, dreading with each step what he will find when he reaches his home. His worst fears are realized when he finally arrives late in the afternoon; most of his village has been burnt to the ground; bodies lie everywhere. Traumatized by what he has found, tears stream down the shaman's face as he walks amongst the remains of his people. He sees everyone: the children he saved from sickness, the mothers he helped through childbirth, the young men he'd cared for from the time they were born. Then he discovers the body of his chief, and with him, the bodies of his two sons, Elike and Mawuko, their weapons still in their hands.

Overcome with grief and overwhelmed by uncontrollable rage, the shaman decides to seek revenge. In the twilight he sacrifices a goat. After draining the animal's warm blood into a large clay bowl, the shaman takes out the small talisman, which he plunges into the bowl and bathes in blood. The blood of the goat runs down the shaman's arms, as he holds the talisman up over the bodies of his people. He beckons them to rise once more, to rise and take up their weapons, to rise for one last battle. As the shaman chants, the lifeless corpses of the villagers begin to twitch and convulse. A dead child slowly climbs back to her feet as the corpse of her mother takes her place beside the dead girl. The body of the chief begins to awaken as his dead son Elike stands with his spear in his hands. One by one, as the shaman continues to chant, the reanimated bodies of the villagers all rise to their feet.

"Go now!" the shaman commands. "Go swiftly into the darkness! Seek out those who took your lives and take theirs without mercy! Go now and fight! Do not return until you have killed every one of them!"

Propelled by the powerful energy emanating from the talisman, the shaman's deadly zombie army flees into the night. He watches with satisfaction as they disappear into the darkness, then he goes to find digging tools; he has many graves to prepare.

Three days later, the shaman is digging the last of their graves when his zombie army returns. They not only slaughtered the village of the rival chief, but all of the neighboring villages who had aligned with him, murdering every man, woman, and child. Their grim mission of revenge complete, they have returned, drawn back to their home village by the power of the talisman.

9

Silently, the zombie villagers gather before the shaman, who has one last command for them: to rest. Holding up the talisman once more, he sends his reanimated corpses to seek their graves, to find their resting place. One by one the zombie villagers climb down into the holes the shaman dug for them. The shaman watches as Elike, his brother and sisters, his mother and father all quietly lie down in their graves. Once all of his people have been put to rest, the shaman releases the spell, severing each body's bond with the talisman.

The next morning, after he has toiled through the night to cover the last of the graves, the shaman pauses. He takes one last look at his village, and tries to picture in his mind what it looked like when it was a living, vibrant, and prosperous place. He lets the shovel drop from his blistered hands, then picks up his satchel and places the talisman inside it. The shaman turns towards the rising sun and walks off into the empty grassland without looking back.

Chapter 1

Of all the unpleasant characteristics expressed by mankind, perhaps none is more distasteful, more frivolous, yet potentially more damaging than pure vanity. With regard to wildlife, specifically man's personal relationship with wildlife, it is ultimately vanity that is responsible for more extinctions than any other human trait...

Leaning back in his chair, Dr. Peter Marsh pushes his glasses up and rubs his eyes, adjusting the frames, he stares again at the glowing display in front of him. The words he's just written stare back blankly. He knows he still doesn't have it right, but he'll leave them there for now. He's six months into a twelve-month research grant to study the effects of collapsing shark populations, focusing his efforts within a region stretching from the Philippine Sea, west across the Luzon Strait and into a section of the South China Sea. He and his team are aboard the privately funded research vessel *Fearless*. Winning the grant had been a major coup, drawing both respect, as well as envy from his colleagues.

Considered the premiere vessel of her kind, *Fearless* is no converted trawler. She was purpose built. At ninety-seven meters, or three hundred and eighteen feet, she is amongst the largest of the active research fleet; however, she's no treasure hunter. *Fearless* is a state-of-the-art, modern vessel devoted purely to science. Over the course of his time on board, Marsh has taken full advantage of the extraordinary opportunities she offers. Along with his team, he's managed to publish three papers so far, an amazing accomplishment in itself. Marsh and his team have been documenting the decline of commercial fisheries as a direct result of severe reductions in the region's shark population. The papers managed to generate considerable buzz within the scientific community, which, politely speaking, means they were actually read by more than one hundred people.

After eighteen years as a leading shark biologist, however, Marsh has not only been writing for science, he's also been writing for himself. Writing in a way that would never be seriously considered by his colleagues who peer review the journals, writing from the heart, and with passion. For the book he's been quietly working on, he wanted to go back to the beginning, back to when he was a boy growing up in Opua, in northern New Zealand's Bay of Islands. Back to a time when his love for the sea and all the life in it was his sole existence.

As a researcher, however, he is expected to set aside emotions, as they are considered impediments to serious scientific study. But over the years, he's found that completely suppressing the passion that drives him leaves him dead inside. So rather than purge emotion completely, he's decided to preserve his deepest feelings in a way that can be shared without judgements. Marsh yawns, stretches, and then glances at the thick dive watch strapped to his left arm. It's late; instinctively he reaches for his favorite mug only to find nothing inside but a withered brown teabag dried to the bottom. He sighs, places the mug back on his desk, shuts down his computer, and goes to bed.

* * *

Mid-morning, and the ship's a hive of activity. Alex Moss, chief of operations, is in his element, which means he's in full problem-solving mode. He's been up for ten hours already, supervising the overnight repositioning of *Fearless* to within helicopter range of shore. In this case, near one of the Babuyan Islands scattered amongst the Philippines' northern Luzon archipelago. Another marine scientist is arriving today, Dr. Thomas Falcon, a British citizen born in Jamaica, and a renowned expert on tropical shark species. He's also a close friend of Dr. Peter Marsh; they attended Cambridge together, but at the moment none of this means dick to Moss. He doesn't work for Dr. Marsh, however, the people he does work for have given him orders to assist the scientists in any way possible, so that's what he'll do. But as far as he's concerned, Falcon is just another *fish doctor*.

As usual there have been issues to deal with. The ship's helicopter, a Bell 429 GlobalRanger, has been grounded for maintenance. Along with his chief pilot, the Bell is currently sitting in a hanger back in Manila waiting for parts. Meanwhile, the local chopper Moss chartered to fill in crashed two days ago while carrying a load of tourists on a sightseeing excursion. So Moss did what he always does; he improvised. Calling in a favor from one of his military buddies, he arranged for Falcon to be transferred to the recently reopened U.S. Naval base at Subic Bay where he'll hitch a ride aboard a Navy chopper that happens to be heading this way. The only catch being that the military helicopter is too big to land on the research vessel's helipad. So Falcon will have to be lowered down by cable-winch while the chopper hovers above deck, a tricky operation, but nothing Moss hasn't managed a hundred times before.

Alex Moss stands calmly on the bridge of *Fearless*. His six foot four frame fills one of the front windows. Well past forty, he still works out every morning at five. His trim muscular physique belies his age; only the graying temples give him away. Now that everything is in place, however, his team is relaxed. Moss lifts his binoculars and squints as he adjusts the focus. "Here she comes," he says, picking up the ship's comm and speaking in a crisp emotionless tone. "Chopper's approaching. All hands prepare for arrival."

First Mate Malcolm Rafferty is supervising operations down on the helipad. Rafferty, like Moss, is a former Navy SEAL who served in Iraq, Afghanistan, and a few other off the books locations, with Moss being four classes ahead of Rafferty in SEAL training. The thirty-nine-year-old Rafferty considers Moss to be not only his closest friend, but a mentor. As the chopper's hulking fuselage darkens the sky above the helipad, a torrent of prop wash causes the crew on deck to momentarily lose their balance. Rafferty stands firm, however, his hands on his hips as he looks up at the chopper crew preparing to lower the basket containing Dr. Falcon. He can hear Moss through his radio headset: "Razz, you got that fish doctor in sight? Are we all go?"

"Ax, roger that, we are all go, fish doc deployed. They're lowering the basket now; we have fish in a basket."

The basket is halfway down when a gust of wind briefly catches it, causing it to spin. The crew in the chopper quickly compensate, but this causes the rescue basket to spin back again in order to right itself. The chopper ride out from the naval base had not been a pleasant trip to begin with for Dr. Thomas Falcon. Now, inside the spinning basket, poised precariously above the moving deck of a ship at sea, Falcon is wishing he'd skipped lunch.

As the basket descends towards them, Rafferty and his three-man deck crew must quickly position its grounding cable before they can safely grab the basket's stainless steel frame. To do otherwise would result in a nasty jolt of highly charged static electricity. The operation goes smoothly, and as the basket comes within reach, the men grab hold of it, guiding it until it touches down. Swiftly and professionally, they pull Falcon and his gear from the basket, release it, and in seconds the Navy helicopter is up and back on its way. On his feet, Falcon is suddenly overcome by a wave of severe nausea just as Alex Moss and Dr. Marsh step onto the helipad to greet him.

"Tom!" Marsh calls out. "It's great to see you."

At that moment Falcon doubles over, spraying the helipad with vomit. Moss looks down at the mess splattered across his deck shoes. "Ah, I see it was taco day at the base."

Chapter 2

Some forty miles southwest of the current position of *Fearless*, another vessel is hard at work, her crew plying their trade as shark fishermen aboard a Chinese fin trawler. Finning, as it is known, has grown into a highly lucrative business over the past twenty years as China has awakened, and risen, into a capitalistic industrial super power. Along with her unprecedented economic growth has come an ever-expanding class of extremely wealthy *nouveau riche*, all of whom are now demanding the accouterments appropriate to their newfound status. One of these being the ability to host lavish banquets for weddings and other social events where serving shark fin soup to three hundred guests is considered an impressive expression of privilege, generosity, and good fortune.

Dating back over a thousand years, the dish was once amongst the exclusive cuisine of emperors, but these days, it's no longer reserved for royalty. Anyone can have shark fin, that is, if they're willing to pay the price. It's one of the *big four*, a complement of four traditional delicacies included within a menu of twelve or more dishes. Served, not so much for how they taste, as for what they represent. There is *Boa*, or abalone, and *Shen*, otherwise known as sea cucumber, then arrives *Du*, or fish maw, but always topping the list is *Yú Chì*, the shark fin, which is considered the most auspicious.

The dried fin is reconstituted in a complex broth, the shark fin itself having almost no flavor. It is the texture that is the most sought after and desired; stringy, gelatinous, with an appearance like hand-cut pasta. The fanciest, most expensive version contains an entire fin in each bowl. The flesh is white, delicately fanned out like a flower, yet echoes the sweeping shape of the fin itself. Demand is high, and so are the prices paid for top-quality shark fin, but there's just one problem; the oceans are quickly running out of sharks.

For the crew of this particular fin trawler though, it's been a good week. In just the past few days they've processed nearly two thousand sharks, all in a relatively small area. After chumming the water and running their nets in a circular pattern, the crew begin hauling in their catch. The trawler's rusted winches protest loudly under the strain as the heavy load is brought on board. Once the net is opened, the workers on deck coldly begin the grim task of slicing away the fins of the struggling sharks. As each animal is mutilated, more crewmen callously hook into their bodies with long gaffs and toss what's left overboard.

Sharks have been fished for centuries. Traditionally, the entire fish is taken, and every part of the animal can be legally marketed: the meat, the liver and cartilage, the hide for its leather, as well as the fins. With the sharp rise in demand driving the exorbitant price of shark fin, however, an illicit practice has risen whereby fishermen are only interested in the highly valuable fins; no other part of the shark is harvested.

The fins take up very little space on board, allowing even a modest vessel to accumulate thousands during a run. The sharks themselves are very much alive during the entire ordeal. Once thrown back, the ocean that was once theirs to command has now turned against them as they suddenly find they can no longer swim. Fighting a losing battle for their lives, the crippled sharks sink helplessly to the bottom in a heap where they die a slow and painful death. With another day's work complete, the crew pull in their remaining nets, clean them of bycatch, and move on.

• • •

The following morning, Dr. Peter Marsh is sitting alone in the crew mess having his usual breakfast: organic oatmeal, plain yogurt, fresh fruit, and a cup of black tea, no sugar, when Dr. Falcon walks in. The sight of Marsh eating suddenly leaves him queasy.

"I thought I could handle some food, but I think I've changed my mind."

"Tom!" Marsh calls to his friend. "You are looking a bit out of sorts, but nothing a cuppa can't fix. I'll have the kitchen send one out. A touch of milk, no sugar, right?"

"You do remember everything, don't you?" Falcon manages a smile, then he comically takes on a mocking posh accent: "Oh yes dear, do have the kitchen help send something out…" Falcon chuckles, then shifts to a more serious tone. "I saw the lab, oh excuse me, I mean labs… and this ship! She's amazing, absolutely bonkers! You could serve meals in the engine room, and the dive deck is positively enormous. Let's see, what else… oh the infirmary is incredible. I can't believe this ship actually has a surgical suite, and its own X-ray machine? That's just unheard of. Peter, my word, they have a hyperbaric chamber; I've never seen so much splashy kit. The last research boat I worked on had little more than a packet of plasters and some gauze… But my absolute favorite bit by far has to be the submarine. What a beautiful machine."

Marsh cuts in: "A UBW C-Researcher 3, no less, built in the Netherlands. You know that beauty has a max depth of seventeen-hundred meters?"

"She is magnificent," Falcon agrees. "Maybe I'll get to dust off the old submersible license, see if I still have the touch. But *Fearless*? Who comes up with a name like that?"

"Americans."

"Right."

"So I see you enjoyed the tour then. It must have started early."

"Commenced promptly at 0700 sharp."

"Let me guess, with Mr. Rafferty?"

"What is it they call these blokes? *Jarheads*?"

"Hush man," Marsh quickly responds. "You'll ring hell down on us for that. Jarheads are Marines; most of the Neanderthals you see around here are former Navy SEALs, what the military types call *special operations forces*. SEAL stands for Sea, Air, and Land; you know, as in *SEAL Team Six*. For all we know, some of these men may have taken out Osama bin Laden himself."

"So I guess that makes Mr. Moss chief Neanderthal?"

"He's a good man, actually. I've come to respect Alex Moss a great deal. He works directly for the foundation that funds all of this…" Marsh pauses momentarily while he waves his hands in small circles as if he were the Pope giving a blessing. "I've been told the ship's annual operating budget is over thirty million U.S. dollars; it's an enormous responsibility. After six months on board, I can tell you the man's exceptional at his job. He runs a very tight ship, the best I've ever had the privilege to work on."

"Well then, I guess we'd better get to work, show the Foundation they've spent their money well."

* * *

In the four days since Falcon's dramatic arrival aboard *Fearless*, he and Marsh have spent the bulk of their time in the ship's state-of-the-art research lab going over the raw data the team have been collecting. Falcon is well versed on the issues; he's been following Marsh's published research from the beginning, but it's the more recent, unpublished data he's most interested in seeing. When Marsh invited him to join his team for the remainder of the season, he jumped at the chance to get out of his own meager university lab and back into the field. The opportunity to work with a close friend made the offer all the more attractive.

On a personal level, Falcon saw this as a chance to actually do something, to make a physical contribution toward conservation, not just publish papers. As Marsh and Falcon look at a large flat screen monitor, complex modeling software is processing the latest inputs. Marsh pauses the program, then glances up at Falcon. "What you are looking at is the most recent data we've compiled, and we got it by directly tracking the finning boats."

"Once we've located a kill-zone," Marsh continues, "we dive directly on the site, and make a survey of the number of sharks killed; we pay careful attention to what species we find. The radar systems aboard *Fearless* are the most sophisticated I've ever seen. The fin boats try to avoid detection, of course, but we've found that when they're laying out their nets, they leave a tell-tale signature. Frankly, I'm shocked at how many there actually are out there. At the moment, we're working to generate precise estimates of the depletion rates of adult breeding populations in the region around the Luzon Strait, and specifically, to track the decline of rare species."

Falcon looks intently at the screen and then begins taking notes. "What kind of numbers are we talking about here, Peter? How bad is it really?"

Marsh raises up from the screen, then turns to look at Falcon. "Based on what we've collected so far, we estimate a half million sharks have been taken in this quadrant alone since we began our survey six months ago. At this rate, within five years there won't be a single shark alive in this entire region."

Falcon is stunned into silence, struggling to comprehend what Marsh has just told him, but the silence is interrupted when Moss enters the lab. "The sub just returned from this morning's reconnaissance; they're downloading the images now. The pilot says it's the worst he's ever seen. Based on what he's told me, you'll want to get your team ready for the next count."

Down on the dive deck, Falcon, Marsh, and his two graduate student assistants, Brian and Alistair, are in full SCUBA, preparing to dive one hundred feet down to the area the sub has just finished mapping and photographing. After reviewing the digital images and video, the two scientists agree with the sub's pilot; it's possibly the worst kill-zone any of them have ever encountered. Malcolm Rafferty will lead the dive, while Moss, as always, will stay with the ship.

Rafferty gives the pre-dive briefing. "Maximum depth is thirty meters, maximum bottom time will be seventeen minutes, no exceptions, gentlemen, so use the time wisely."

The five divers stand in formation as the ship's hydraulic dive platform slowly lowers to the sea. Rafferty then signals for the first pair to deploy, followed by the second, then he follows. Descending down through the clear tropical water, Falcon is reminded of his home in the Caribbean. At forty feet, the vast reef below becomes visible. On any other dive, Falcon would be elated at this point, filled with anticipation, but not this time. He glances over at Marsh as the first carcasses come into view; Marsh just shakes his head. The stark white corpses are scattered everywhere. Looking down from above, they resemble a box of toothpicks that has been spilled onto the floor.

Once on the bottom, however, Falcon and Marsh are overcome by the sheer scale of destruction all around them. The landscape is a wasteland of hundreds upon hundreds of decaying shark carcasses, but the two scientists know this is no time to allow emotion to gain control, so they go to work. The group fans out to begin cataloging the precisely mapped section of the kill-zone they'd previously selected, recording the various shark species they find inside the grid in order to project as accurate a picture as possible of the entire area.

As the team carefully sorts through the pile of corpses by hand, they find the fishermen play no favorites. They will record fourteen different species. Among them: black tip, silver tip, an oceanic white tip, three nurse sharks, two scalloped hammerheads, a bull shark, a leopard shark, several grey reef sharks, a lemon shark… then Falcon circles a large coral formation and comes across an enormous tiger shark, a female, her once magnificent body now savaged and mutilated, overwhelmed. He begins to weep.

Chapter 3

Back on board, Marsh supervises as Brian and Alistair, his graduate students, input the data the team has just collected. Falcon is assisting as best he can, but the shock of what he's just witnessed is hindering his professional ability. He can't concentrate. He's as angry at himself over his inability to control his emotions as he is disappointed in his lack of a meaningful contribution to the project. Marsh can clearly see the distress on his friend's face. "The first time is always the hardest," he comforts. "But the better we do our job, the faster we can do something to stop this."

Later that night Falcon is alone in his cabin, and finds himself struggling with overwhelming rage. *Why am I even here?* he asks himself. *What sort of meaningful contribution can I possibly make?* Searching for some form of emotional comfort, something positive to focus his mind on, he pulls out his duffle bag. Falcon reaches inside to retrieve a carved wooden box. The box contains an assortment of mementos he carries with him wherever he goes.

From inside he lifts out a faded photograph, a picture of himself at age seven taken in Jamaica. In the photo he's smiling broadly, sitting on the lap of his grandmother. She has her arms around him, holding him close. The photo was taken thirty-five years ago, but looking at it makes Falcon feel as if it were just yesterday. In the photo, his grandmother is wearing a distinctive necklace. At its center is a small, well-worn statue carved from bone.

It looked as if it had once been carved to depict some sort of antelope, but years of wear have made the designs almost unreadable. The statue is more than a piece of antique folk art, however. It's a Vodun talisman, carried by an ancestor to Jamaica from West Africa. Falcon's grandmother had always claimed her family descended from a long line of Vodun shamans, and that the talisman was actually eight hundred years old. Falcon sets the photo aside. Then, opening the box again, he lifts out the talisman itself, then unwraps it from the tissue it had been stored inside.

Holding it in his hand, he recalls what his grandmother told him the night she gave the talisman to him. It was just before he left home to attend university in England… "There is great power in this spirit," she said. "The power of life, power to prevent death, and power over death. Handle this carefully; keep it with you always; never let it leave you."

As a boy, Falcon had loved listening to his grandmother's stories of the Vodun spirits. How their divine essence governs the earth, the sea, and all of its creatures. As a scientist, however, he had dismissed them long ago as just that: stories. Now, consumed with despair and anger, Falcon decides he should use the talisman. If there truly is any power in this spirit, as his grandmother claimed, perhaps there's a chance it might free him from his anger and allow him to do his job: to be a scientist. Falcon tucks the talisman inside his pocket, grabs his smokes, his lighter, and goes outside.

He heads down to the far aft deck of the ship, just above the dive deck. This is the only place onboard anyone can smoke. Although, technically speaking, there's a ship-wide smoking ban issued by Moss himself. But some of the more dedicated smokers on board have found a way to sidestep Moss and his smoking ban. There are usually a few guys hanging out back there, and sure enough, Falcon finds two crewmen. He shares his cigarettes with them, they chat for a bit, then leave. Once the aft deck is clear of potential witnesses, Falcon draws in one last long drag, then snuffs out his cigarette. Making his way down to the dive deck, he grabs a full tank, regulator, fins, mask, and a weight belt. He forgoes the wetsuit, as a soggy one left on deck is a sure giveaway. He then rigs up the gear for a dive.

Fearless is still at anchor, still positioned over the kill-zone when Falcon slips into the moonlit sea. He descends down into the inky darkness, allowing his eyes to adjust. Using a dive light would give him away instantly, so he dives by moonlight instead. The darker indigo splotches of reef become visible first, contrasted sharply against the pale blue of the white sand bottom. Then the eerie forms of the dead sharks come into view. Their mutilated bodies form a landscape of death as far as he can see in all directions. Falcon freezes. Suspended in watery space, panic starts to take hold. His breathing increases, sending a flurry of bubbles rapidly spewing from his regulator. He can feel his heart rate accelerating; he's on the edge of losing control. Instinctively, he reaches down to his pocket and feels the talisman. His breathing slows, as his heart rate drops back to normal; he continues his descent.

Once on the bottom, he retraces the exact path he'd made during the morning dive. Then Falcon spots the distinctive coral formation he'd seen before, and there, just where he'd found her the first time, lay the massive lifeless corpse of the female tiger shark. Falcon strokes her tenderly while remembering an ancient prayer his grandmother had taught him. Then he takes the Vodun talisman from his pocket and carefully places it inside her huge gaping jaws. Falcon's hope is that with this small gesture, he might free the spirit of the shark, and also himself.

Ascending back to the surface, Falcon's slim silhouette is bathed in shafts of silver moonlight. He can see the outline of *Fearless* clearly, her twin anchor chains trailing off from her bow into the dark sea. As he surfaces, he's overcome by a sense of peace; he feels certain he's done the right thing. Making his way back to the dive platform, he finds the rope he'd left tied there. He uses it to hoist himself back onto the raised dive deck. Then he carefully wipes down all of the gear he'd used and returns it back to its designated storage. Placing the now-empty tank in its holder, he leaves the valve open; perhaps someone will think it was an oversight.

* * *

Meanwhile, far below, a strange energy has begun to spread across the entirety of the kill-zone. A powerful force now emanates from the body of the female tiger shark. The ancient power builds slowly at first as her tail begins to twitch. Then, as the energy field gains strength, the tiger shark's body rapidly convulses. Then her dead white eyes suddenly shift, as her jaws slowly close around the talisman that is feeding her false life. Nearby, a large lemon shark also begins to twitch, then another, while a black tip shark fiercely wriggles and thrashes against the bodies piled on top of it.

The power rapidly increases, reanimating the entire kill-zone of shark corpses. All of them now begin to twitch and thrash, tumbling over each other as the energy field locks onto each and every one of them and takes control of their bodies. Their decomposed corpses have been ignited by the power of the talisman. A zombie horde has been awakened, propelled by the energy radiating out from the female tiger shark. Fully upright, she begins to rise from the bottom, and leading an army raised from pure death, the zombie shark horde streaks off into the darkness.

* * *

Nineteen miles due south of their last position, the Chinese fin trawler has had another highly profitable day. So good in fact, the captain has kept the crew working late into the night. It's well past midnight, and the nets are out again, making their circles of death. When the crew suddenly takes in an enormous haul, they excitedly call out to the captain, who is standing above them on the catwalk outside the boat's deckhouse. "We have the biggest catch ever!" they shout. "We're all getting paid double, right?"

The ship's winches can hardly handle the load as the fishermen's bounty is maneuvered onto the kill deck. Then the net is opened, and the sharks spill out, their bodies sliding out across the grimy, blood-soaked steel plating. The mostly Filipino crew all suddenly leap back, and several draw their hands to their noses as a deep rotting stench fills the air. Others drop their knives and run, while still others, frozen in terror, begin to cross themselves, praying to God for mercy.

"What has happened? Get back to work, you shits!" the captain shouts down from the deckhouse.

"But captain, look! These sharks are already dead! They have no fins to cut!"

"You stupid shits!" The captain pauses momentarily, peering down from the railing. "You've hauled in sharks we've already processed. Get rid of them! Get those nets back in the water, you dumb shits!"

The crew grab their gaffs, and begin hooking into the decomposed bodies of the finless sharks, dragging them back overboard. One crewmen swings his gaff, plunging it into a very large, very dead tiger shark. As the sharp hook of the gaff strikes flesh, instantly the shark lunges at him, taking the crewmen's right arm into her jaws. Screaming in terror, the crewman looks down as the shark then violently shakes her head, her teeth savagely tearing into his flesh. The force knocks him off his feet as she slings him back and forth across the deck. The other men quickly come to the aid of their shipmate, attempting to beat the shark off with their gaffs, but the zombie tiger shark is unaffected. She is nothing but a reanimated corpse. She has no life to lose, no fear of injury, and no sense of self-preservation.

As the crewmen attempt to fight off the tiger shark's attack, she continues unaffected. Trapped in the grip of her massive jaws, the desperate man pounds her head with his fist, kicking at lifeless flesh in a futile attempt to escape as the shark's teeth relentlessly saw their way through muscle, then bone, and with a loud snap, rip away the man's arm just below the shoulder.

Chaos flash-burns through the men left facing the zombie horde when another crewmen shrieks in agony as a lemon shark sinks its teeth into his upper thigh, releasing a fountain of blood gushing down his legs. The deck of the fin boat is once again awash in blood, but this time it's human blood, as the zombie sharks launch into a full force attack.

In blind panic, many crewmen jump overboard, only to find the sea they've leapt into is a churning froth of viciously snapping jaws, eager to shred them to bits as soon as the men touch water. The captain meanwhile has fled the catwalk and locked himself inside the deckhouse. He begins to send out a radio distress call, but the deckhouse windows are suddenly shattered as two zombie black tip sharks crash through. They land directly at the feet of the captain. The radio handset drops from his hands as he steps back against the ship's control panel. The two black tip sharks are snapping madly as the captain scrambles for anything that might serve as a weapon but finds nothing. As the zombie sharks' jaws move like buzz saws toward him, the captain pisses himself and the sharks attack.

Chapter 4

Alex Moss is not having a good morning. Something on board his ship is out of place. On board *his* ship, things are not as they should be. A thorough grilling of the crew has yielded nothing useful other than the fact that he needs to tighten up on his no-smoking policy. Moss reckons the culprit is amongst the science team, but it doesn't make sense. The situation doesn't add up, and when things don't add up, Moss won't rest until they do. Marsh and Falcon are in the main computer lab processing data when Moss interrupts them. "Sorry to bother you, gentlemen, but can I ask you a few questions? We have a minor equipment issue we're trying to clear up."

Marsh looks at Falcon, who shrugs, then they both look at Moss. "Of course, Mr. Moss, ask away," says Marsh.

"Anything we can help you with, no worries," adds Falcon.

"It appears we had an unauthorized dive take place last night," Moss announces calmly.

Marsh looks stunned, while Falcon's expression is flat, completely neutral. Moss pauses for a moment; he's not reading anything unusual off these guys, but he's not giving up just yet. "We found an empty tank. All of our dive tanks are numbered and precisely catalogued for maintenance purposes. Our records show this particular tank had been inspected, refilled and placed back in the ready service dock. There's no way that tank could be empty unless someone used it."

Marsh looks directly at Moss. "I'm not sure what I can tell you, Mr. Moss. I don't know anything about it." He then turns to Falcon. "How about you, Tom?"

Falcon glances at Marsh, then looks directly at Moss, his rock solid poker face giving nothing away. "I'm afraid I have nothing useful to contribute here either. I must apologize, I wish I could be more help."

Moss, processing every movement, every word the two men tell him, is still getting no signal. "If it's all right with you, Dr. Marsh, I'd like to question the rest of your team. I run a safe ship here; I don't want anyone getting hurt."

"By all means, Mr. Moss. We're at your disposal."

At that moment the ship's radar proximity alarm goes off, signaling a threat has entered the radar systems guard zone. Moss doesn't hesitate; he bolts from the lab, then sprints up the stairs toward the bridge.

Moss and Rafferty enter the bridge at the same time. "Razz, how can this happen? Where the hell's the watch crew?" Moss shouts. Heading for the window, he spots the approaching vessel: white, with a distinctive orange and blue stripe across her bow. "It's ok; it looks like the local Coast Guard."

"Who the fuck was on watch?" Rafferty growls as he shuts off the alarm, then grabs the duty roster.

Moss sighs. "Better get our documents out of the safe; it's probably just a spot inspection."

The Philippine Coast Guard cutter pulls up a short distance from *Fearless*, then radios a request to board immediately, which Moss grants. As the boarding party approaches, Moss is waiting for them. Rafferty is standing nearby, holding the ship's paperwork and crew passports in a waterproof pouch. Both Moss and Rafferty are wearing their standard crew uniforms: white polo shirts embroidered with the *Fearless Research Foundation* logo, navy blue Bermuda shorts, and deck shoes. The cutter's second in command greets Moss politely as he steps onto the deck of *Fearless* for the first time.

"From the moment I first saw her, I have wanted to see this ship up close," the officer announces. "I wish it was under better circumstances. Is there some place we can speak privately?" Moss glances at Rafferty, who knows whatever is going on, it has nothing to do with paperwork. Moss then shows the officer to his personal office.

"Can I get you anything, sir? Coffee, tea? Would you care to sit down?" The officer is clearly uncomfortable, nervous even. Moss senses fear from this man, the sort that tells him something serious has happened.

"No, thank you for your hospitality, sir but… this is highly irregular but, we would like to ask for your help."

"Of course, absolutely. What can I do for you?"

"You are a science vessel, correct? You currently have a team on board that specializes in sharks?"

"Some of the best in the world, sir."

"There's been an incident. We're not sure what to make of it just yet. We are in the process of gathering more information, and this of course is why I am here speaking with you now, Mr. Moss. We received a partial distress call from a commercial fishing boat early this morning at approximately 0300. We dispatched a rescue vessel to intercept; they found the fishing boat adrift. All of her crew appear to be dead."

"I'm not sure how we can help, sir; sounds more like a possible pirate assault. Maybe drug traffickers?"

"We're coming to you for help, Mr. Moss, because of the way the men died; their bodies were found severely mutilated, as if attacked by sharks."

"If you give us the coordinates of the fishing boat, we'll go check it out."

"We can do better than that, Mr. Moss. We'll escort you there ourselves."

Later that afternoon, *Fearless*, escorted by the Philippine Coast Guard, arrives at the coordinates of the fishing boat. A smaller Coast Guard vessel is already rafted up alongside. Her crew had been there all morning conducting their investigation and guarding the stricken vessel to prevent any other boats from approaching. Now they are under orders to halt their investigation and wait for the arrival of the science team from *Fearless*. Moss, Rafferty, Falcon, and Marsh are given hazmat gear and ferried over to the fishing boat along with the Coast Guard cutter's second in command and two of his crew. Upon arrival on board the Chinese fishing boat, Marsh and Falcon are both immediately sickened by the gruesome scene that confronts them.

"My god, I can't look at this," says Marsh.

"Once again, I should have skipped lunch," quips Falcon,

"Have some respect, Tom. These men died horrifically; they had families,"

"Sorry, it's a defensive reflex. You're right, of course."

Meanwhile Moss and Rafferty solemnly move through the carnage, each showing no emotion as they make careful observations. Both men are intensely mindful to avoid stepping on anything that looks like human blood or flesh. The aftermath looks painfully familiar to them. They've both seen this sort of thing far too many times before.

"If I didn't know better…" starts Rafferty,

"Yeah, looks like an IED attack to me too," adds Moss.

"Is that a head over there?"

"Half of one at least." Moss pauses momentarily, then looks at Rafferty. "This is all very strange Razz— too strange. There's nothing here, other than the remains themselves that tells me any sort of explosives were used."

"My thoughts exactly," adds Rafferty. "I mean, look at this boat: there's no structural damage. I see no evidence of small arms fire, no hull damage that might indicate an impact of some sort, not even fire damage. What the hell did this?"

Moss stops in his tracks. Placing his hands on his hips, he exhales in disgust as he stares out at the horizon. "I don't know, but whatever it was, let's hope we don't get to see it up close."

Marsh and Falcon have composed themselves enough to begin their own investigation. Falcon finds a severed arm lying in the sun, an arm with telltale wounds he's seen before. He motions Marsh over to take a closer look.

"Peter, I know what I'm thinking, but what do you make of this?" Falcon uses his gloved hands to carefully turn the arm over.

"Well," says Marsh, bending down and then adjusting his glasses. "These serrated lacerations are certainly consistent with a shark bite. I've analyzed the data from hundreds of shark attacks, and judging by this jagged pattern, I would say it was most certainly a rather large specimen that took this poor chap's arm off so viciously. Honestly, though, none of this makes sense, Tom. I mean, we're on the deck of a fishing boat. How did a man get his arm bitten off on deck?"

"Peter, look around you. This is no ordinary fishing boat. Look at that gear over there; look at all these knives lying about. This is a fin boat, Peter. These guys were finning, and it looks to me like for once, the sharks may have won this battle."

"Oh, come on, Tom, be serious! Yes, you're right," Marsh admits, he glances to one side of the boat, then the other. "Now that you mention it, this is, or was, a finning operation. Certainly a man can be bitten, even lose his arm while slicing the fins off large sharks, but the whole crew, Tom? How can this be? The Coast Guard officer told me they found the captain of this boat torn to shreds in the deckhouse, Tom—*inside the deckhouse...* How could a shark do that? You and I both know it's impossible."

Just then Moss and Rafferty approach. Moss is carrying a small plastic bag. "The Coast Guard medical officer gave us these; he thought you two would want to examine them." He hands the bag to Marsh.

Marsh lifts the bag up in front of his face. "These are fresh shark teeth. Where did they find these?"

"He told me he had been digging them out of the remains all morning."

Chapter 5

Thirty miles to the south, an exclusive island beach resort has become a fashionable, newfound hideaway. It is the prime season, and the resort's super-chic oceanfront bungalows are brimming with the rich and famous, while its pristine, powder white-sand beach is a hive of activity as neatly uniformed waitstaff scurry about, attending to guests accustomed to high-priced pampering. A young waitress politely places an exotic cocktail on the side-table of a man who is sunbathing alongside his third wife. He's twenty years her senior; she's a former model. He leans over to inspect the drink.

"Crap, not again. I said no cherries!" he barks as the young woman tries to apologize for the mistake. "Don't you people speak English? Take it back!"

"Darling, what's wrong?" His wife attempts to comfort him, but he brushes her off.

"Forget it. I'm going for a swim."

* * *

Forty minutes later, the man's wife is walking along the beach searching for her husband when she sees two young lifeguards. The two teens, eighteen and nineteen, have a set of binoculars out, and are busily scanning the surf, watching bikini-clad girls jumping about in the waves.

"Come on, it's my turn," one says to the other in the local dialect.

"Excuse me, gentlemen…"

The two boys are startled; one drops the binoculars in the sand. "I can't seem to locate my husband. He went swimming almost an hour ago, and I haven't seen him since."

The two teens look at each other, then the older of the pair nervously stammers in dialect, "Oh shit! That's the third one in the past twenty minutes!"

"What do we do?" The younger of the two has only been on the job a couple of weeks. "We're gonna get fired, man!"

Then the older boy realizes reluctantly that he should take charge. "It could be a swarm of jellyfish? If it is, more people could get injured. We should call the office, and I think we should close the beach. We need to clear all of these people out of here, so we can search for the ones that are missing."

The wife can't understand the lifeguards' rapid exchange, but the way they're speaking worries her. She can clearly see the boys are nervous about something. "What's wrong? Is something going on? Can you speak to me in English, please?"

"Lady, please," the older boy says in English as he tries to sound calm. "We will find your husband, but we must clear the beach. Please go wait for him in the hotel, ok?"

The two lifeguards grab their whistles and initiate a meek attempt to clear the crowded beach, but soon realize they might as well be blowing whistles at a football match. The older boy pulls a handheld radio from his pocket and tries to call up to the main office, when they hear a sudden brief scream. They stop to look, as does everyone else on the beach. The whole place briefly goes silent, but nobody sees anything, so they return to swimming.

The boys start blowing their whistles again, but much more forcefully this time as they now work earnestly to get people out of the water. The few guests paying attention begin wading ashore. A young mother with twin toddlers manages to gather them up and walk out of the water. As she passes her lounge chair, she deftly grabs her beach bag, and, still carrying the twins, heads back to her bungalow. Most of the guests are slow to act, however. They can't understand why, on such a beautiful beach, these two kids are blowing whistles and shouting for them to leave.

Then another scream fills the air, as a woman swimming toward the beach unwittingly collides with the missing husband. Only the upper half of his body is left. It's floating face down in the water; his lower torso and legs have been savagely torn away. The man's intestines, now bobbing loose in the water, have wrapped around the woman's wrist while a rapidly expanding cloud of blood stains the clear tropical water around her.

As the realization sinks in that she's just become entangled in the internal organs of a dead man, the woman begins screaming hysterically. In desperate panic, she thrashes the water as she fights to free herself from the corpse. Other guests gasp around her as they all suddenly realize what's happening. Many more begin to scream, which adds to the building frenzy. Increasing numbers of guests start aggressively pushing their way toward shore, shoving others out of their way, as a viral panic rapidly spreads through the crowd.

Shark! The lone cry is soon joined by others, igniting an incendiary flash of pure fear. The guests quickly succumb to collective terror, until the individuals themselves meld into an unthinking, uncontrollable, yet unified force. In the resulting stampede, the mindless mob crushes anyone slower and struggling. Older people and children are knocked down under the waves as the stronger and faster trample over them. The once-idyllic tropical scene descends into total chaos, the turquoise water suddenly churning to frothy white from a torrent of flailing arms and legs as a crowd of two hundred holiday-makers races toward shore.

The two lifeguards are still blowing their whistles, futilely attempting to regain a sense of order, but it's no use. One of them spots an elderly woman struggling in the surf, and wades out to help her. He nearly has her on her feet when a large dark shape catches his attention. He looks up to see a massive tiger shark. Its huge jaws are wide open; it's leaping out of the water straight at him. Instinctively he dives for the waves, pulling the woman down with him. The shark just misses them, it passes just over their heads and lands a few feet away on the beach.

Jaws snapping wildly, the tiger shark grabs a fleeing man by the leg. Screaming, kicking, and clawing at the sand, the man struggles to break free, but the female zombie tiger shark has him firmly in her grip as she drags her victim into the surf. Nearby a young woman is running for the beach; she's in ankle-deep water when another zombie shark bites down on her foot, yanking her off balance. It then pulls her screaming back into the sea.

Across the beach, just as guests and hotel employees think they've made it to safety, zombie sharks by the hundred now fly out of the surf onto the sand, viciously attacking everyone, violently ripping into human flesh as others run in a stampede of sheer terror. In the midst of it all, the two lifeguards have managed to pull the elderly woman to safety. They each have her by the arm, helping her to run with them up to the main pool area where dozens of tourists have gathered. In shock, the crowd watches an unimaginable horror unfold before their eyes. Some flee, while others stand frozen in disbelief, unable to look away.

From the pool deck somebody begins shouting, "Look! My god, look out there!" On the horizon, a dark undulating line is approaching. A wave is building. Moving towards shore at incredible speed, the wave grows and expands as it approaches. Many think it's a tsunami, as more members of the crowd begin to run away.

The huge building wave then begins to break as it rapidly closes in on the beach. A chilling realization hits onlookers; the wave is not made of water—it's made of sharks. As the rapidly approaching wave of zombie sharks becomes more visible, some still stand transfixed, fascinated even. Others have pulled out their phones in order to record the event. Then the wave crashes on shore, exploding into an unstoppable flood of zombie sharks.

As the zombie horde rockets toward the hotel, the crowd around the pool suddenly shatters, knocking over tables, shoving lounge chairs and umbrellas into the pool as people attempt to escape, somewhere, anywhere. One young man climbs a trellis. As he scrambles to the roof of the building, he then turns to help his girlfriend as she too climbs to the rooftop. He holds her hand tightly as they run to the roof's highest peak then look back. In disbelief they gaze down at what seems like a surreal tableau, as the zombie horde continues to pour out from the sea. As if the horde had no end, it keeps spreading. The wave is unstoppable as it rolls out over the beach, a wall of crazed, snapping jaws rushing right at them.

As a last effort, the young man pulls out his phone in order to leave a message for their families. The lovers then hold on to each other, unable to climb any higher, unable to run anywhere else, and unable to watch as a crescendo of horrific human cries rises from the pool area. They hide their faces in each other's arms as the terrifying sounds fill the air. The zombie sharks relentlessly slaughter everyone in their path, ravaging people's bodies until nothing recognizable remains. Then, inexplicably, as quickly as it appeared, the horde recedes, disappearing back into the sea.

Chapter 6

Fearless is underway. Having received word of the second attack, she's on a direct course, heading toward the resort island in tandem with the Coast Guard cutter. Marsh and Falcon have been working through the night in order to extract viable DNA from the samples of shark teeth they received. They will use the data to identify the species of shark involved in the fishing boat deaths.

"Looks like those last samples we isolated were intact enough to identify what type of shark we're dealing with," says Falcon as he lays the computer printout on the table in front of Marsh,

"Well this is certainly odd," Marsh observes as he picks up an optical loupe, then uses it to examine the printouts. He recognizes some of the patterns immediately; he's seen them many times before.

"According to this…" Marsh's voice trails off as he slides the loupe down the printout. "Mind you, this is just a small sample of what we've collected…"

Falcon breaks in, "Well, don't keep me in suspense, you're far better at reading these things than I am."

Marsh raises up from the table, "From what I can discern, we actually have the DNA of several different species here. It's interesting, but also a bit strange. You see this set of markers here, Tom? That's the DNA of an oceanic white tip, and this one here, those markers are from a tiger shark."

"So we have the DNA of two known man-eaters then," adds Falcon. "We could be on to something here."

"Not so fast," Marsh pulls out the loupe once more, then bends down again to examine the data further. "Yeah, that's what I thought..." His words fade as he concentrates on the pattern, pressing his eye to the loupe as he moves it slowly down the column of data. "This pattern belongs to a leopard shark," Marsh says as he straightens. He then points at the next column of data, "and this one is from a common nurse shark. Neither of these species have ever been recorded killing anyone. They're less likely to bite than your neighbor's poodle."

"So how do you suggest we proceed from here, Peter?"

Marsh looks at Falcon. "I haven't the foggiest, old friend."

* * *

The next day, *Fearless* has dropped anchor along with the Coast Guard cutter. Both ships are within three hundred meters of the beach where the latest attack has taken place. Moss has called a briefing ahead of their planned rendezvous with the Coast Guard on shore. "I've been in communication with the local authorities. They're grateful for any assistance we can lend. Speaking for the Foundation, we now consider this situation to be a potential threat to this ship. Any and all information gathered will be submitted to me personally. Is everyone clear on this? Does everyone understand?"

The group nods in agreement. "I must warn you all ahead of time, this attack resulted in a very high loss of life. Many of the relatives of the hotel employees that were killed are out on that beach as I speak. The local people are treating this area as a grave site. I'm told there are priests here conducting a prayer vigil. The Coast Guard has asked for our utmost discretion and sensitivity when conducting our investigation. The most important piece of news we have is that there are survivors. The police have been interviewing the witnesses. They're going to allow us to ask our own questions, so everybody, keep it brief, keep it professional out there, and stay on task. Now let's get to work."

Moss and Rafferty are joined by Falcon, Marsh, Brian, and Alistair as they motor in toward the beach after launching a rugged inflatable boat (RIB) from *Fearless*. A police forensic team and local coroners are actively working the scene, attempting to recover what's left of the bodies. For the four members of the science team, their anxiety spikes once they have their first full view of the beach in front of them. It is covered in hundreds of small fluttering orange flags, each one marking potential human remains.

As the RIB passes over the hotel's snorkel reef, Marsh glances down into the clear water at the colorful coral lying just below the surface. Suddenly, he sees a face looking back at him. "Wait!" he shouts. "Hold up, I see someone!" The driver cuts the engine and circles back. Moss looks over the side; he can see her... it's part of the body of a young girl, just her upper torso, but her face is clearly visible; she's still wearing her mask and snorkel. "Mark this spot with your GPS," Moss says to Rafferty. His voice is flat, professional, but it's clear he is as affected by what they have just discovered as the others. "Give the coordinates to the forensic team." He sighs. "Let's get to work. I want this over with..."

The RIB continues on toward shore, stopping just short of the beach. Moss and Rafferty immediately climb out of the RIB into shallow water, followed by the science team. Moss orders the driver back to *Fearless*. "I'll radio you when we're ready for pickup." Then he turns to step onto the beach's powder white sand, now stained with patches of oxidized blood. "Don't walk in this," Moss directs, pointing at the blood. Then he looks up toward the hotel's pool area. "I need to speak to the witnesses."

Once again, Marsh and Falcon find they must struggle to compose themselves. The beach is still littered with human remains. Some bodies are covered, while other smaller pieces remain exposed. The two scientists watch as Rafferty and Moss stride off confidently toward the tent the police have erected. Marsh decides to follow the SEALs; he takes Alistair with him.

"Are you coming with us, Tom?"

"I'll catch up to you," Falcon replies. "Mind if I take Brian? We can survey the beach area. Ok with you?"

"Of course," answers Marsh. "Best we split up; we'll cover more ground that way."

The two teams head in opposite directions. Falcon and Brian walk slowly along the beach, looking carefully for any physical evidence left behind by the sharks themselves, when they come across a catholic priest. He is standing knee deep in the water, facing the azure sea and praying for the souls of the dead. His black frock and white tunic slowly drift back and forth in the quiet surf.

As Falcon and Brian watch the priest, Falcon hears a voice behind him. He doesn't understand the language, but something in him, an instinct, says the voice is meant for him. He turns to face the speaker. It's an old man; Falcon has never seen him before, but he recognizes that he's wearing traditional native dress.

Falcon surmises he must be from one of the indigenous tribes that have inhabited these islands for thousands of years. The old man has a boy of about fourteen with him, and the boy approaches Falcon.

"Excuse me, sir, but my grandfather would like to speak to you. He has asked me to translate."

"Of course," replies Falcon. "What can I do for you?"

The old man leans in closely and begins to mutter softly to the young boy. The boy hesitates, but the old man is forceful. Then the boy turns to speak to Falcon as the old man looks intensely into the scientist's eyes.

"My grandfather says to tell you he knows who you are, and what you have done."

"Wha– what?" Falcon is shocked. "What are you talking about?"

"Dr. Falcon," Brian says softly, the young student quietly places his hand on Falcon's shoulder. "Dr. Falcon, the team will be wondering where we are. We'd better go."

"You go on, Brian; I'll be right there." Falcon turns to look at the weathered face of the old man. His eyes do not blink. His expression has not changed; he stares at Falcon with an intensity that vibrates through Falcon's entire body. The boy speaks again,

"My grandfather says to tell you that, although you are a powerful shaman like himself, you were never taught by your ancestors as he was. You have never been shown the true path, and this is why your magic has failed. He says to tell you that you have great pain ahead of you. That many paths now lie in front of you, all of them much more difficult because of your ignorance."

The old man's words hit Falcon as if he were striking him with a cane. The truth in them is undeniable, yet also unbelievable, because they fly against everything the scientist knows and understands.

As Falcon stands frozen in stunned disbelief, the old man continues to softly speak to the boy. "My grandfather says you must seek out the guidance of your ancestors; only they can show you the correct path."

Chapter 7

The team from *Fearless* spent several hours painstakingly working side by side with the local authorities, interviewing witnesses, examining remains, and gathering physical evidence on the beach. The shore party then returned to the ship for some much-needed rest. Falcon is not sleeping, though; he lies in his bunk staring at the ceiling of his cabin. The words of the old shaman keep repeating in his head over and over. *Could it be? Could I possibly have caused all of this?* Then he stops himself. He knows he's just funneling his grief over these tragedies into guilt because he himself has not been directly affected by them. *A classic psychological response*, he tells himself. *Nobody can see what we've seen and not be traumatized by it. It's natural to feel this way, but it's not professional.* He gets up, gets dressed, and goes down to the main lab.

"Can't sleep either?" Peter Marsh comments, as he looks up from his laptop to see Falcon entering the room.

"How can anyone after today?"

Marsh manages a slight smile. "Well, I'm sure the SEALs are all sleeping well. Must be part of their training."

"Yes, of course, the SEALs..." Falcon leans against a lab table attempting to stretch out an awful knot in the base of his spine. Then he straightens up again and looks at Marsh. "You were right, Peter, Mr. Moss is an admirable man. I have to say I've changed my opinion of these guys entirely. The way they can land on a beach, literally surrounded by bloody carnage, and then just go about their job, doing what they came to do without hesitation. I wish I had that ability."

"I know what you mean; I feel the same way, I must admit. But Tom, we're not commandos. We're just a couple of ichthyologists." Marsh suddenly hops up from his chair. "Speaking of science, I've been going over the interview recordings of the witnesses..."

Falcon moves in closer to Marsh. "Those two young lifeguards..."

"Yes, and Mr. Moss agrees with me, those two kids are telling the truth. After comparing their statements against the other witnesses, and as hard as it is for me to get my mind around this, we're clearly dealing with some sort of mass shark attack. A type of behavior completely unknown to science. If we can find evidence to prove this, if our team can document this behavior, then we will have discovered something previously unknown in our field." Marsh sits back down, then he looks up at Falcon, his face filled with uncertainty. "Frankly, Tom, I'm having a very difficult time believing any of this."

"That makes two of us..." Falcon answers. "What about the phone video recorded by that Australian couple on the rooftop? That may be just the evidence we need. It was Mr. Moss who interviewed them, right?"

"That's what we've spent most of our time working on, actually. I downloaded the memory stick the police gave us into the main computer. I've had Brian run it through his video software, trying to clean up the file and enlarge it for more detail. He brought down a fresh rendering about an hour ago. You think you can handle looking at it with me? To tell you the truth, I've held off; I didn't want to look at this alone."

"We're scientists, Peter. We owe it to the families of the victims, we owe it to our colleagues. Let's see what we can find out. Go ahead, run the file."

Spinning around in his chair, Marsh hesitates momentarily in front of the flat screen display, then he hits the space bar on the keyboard, starting the video. It opens with a selfie close-up of the young man's face. The image is handheld, shaky. The girl is only partially in frame; she's sobbing uncontrollably.

"My name is Jonathan Andrew Cummings. I'm on the roof of the Golden Palms resort with my girlfriend Terry Ann Mathewson. We are both from Melbourne. If anyone finds this phone, this video, please let our families know. It's very important people know what's happening here. Please, please let our families know what happened. Mum, Dad, I love you very much."

Then he turns the phone around. He holds it up and aims it down toward the beach. Marsh and Falcon's bodies flinch reflexively as the video focuses on the slaughter taking place at the shoreline. They're instantly repulsed as they can clearly see people being torn apart by hundreds of sharks. Marsh pushes his chair back from the computer, and raises his hands over his mouth.

"My god," says Falcon. "Peter, how can this be possible?"

Then Falcon leans in closer to the screen. "Wait, stop the video. Can we freeze this frame?"

Marsh hits the space bar to stop the video, then begins slowly tapping the backspace key in order to reverse the video frame by frame.

"There, stop it right there. Can we zoom in on that frame a bit more?"

"I can try." Marsh attempts to make the frozen image a bit larger without pixelating it too much. "That's about as good as it's going to get."

Falcon moves in closer, focusing his gaze on the frozen frame. Then his body instantly chills as the blood drains from his face. Marsh watches as his friend stands up, then turns away.

"Tom, what is it? What do you see?" Marsh quickly wipes his glasses, then moves his chair in as close to the screen as he can, his face only inches from the display. "That's a really big shark," Marsh observes, "possibly a tiger, but something's wrong. Where are its fins?"

* * *

It's four-thirty in the morning, and Alex Moss is up as usual, having some coffee and going over paperwork before his workout, when Rafferty knocks on his office door.

"Ax, hey, mind if I disturb you? It was pretty ugly out there yesterday. This situation, it's pretty messed up…" Rafferty pauses as Moss stops what he's doing and looks up.

"Razz I know what you're thinking. I've been thinking the same thing: Whatever attacked that fishing boat, and the resort, whatever it is, it has the ability to attack this ship too. We have to stay on top of this."

Rafferty studies his friend's face. "Have you been in contact with the Foundation? Have you briefed them on the situation?"

"I have," Moss answers, the frustration in his voice evident, "but it's pretty damn difficult to communicate to the board members that we're under threat of attack by a pack of rabid fish, and, frankly, I have a hard time believing this whole thing myself, so how am I going to get them to believe it? They're over seven thousand miles away."

"Are we moving the ship?"

"No, my orders are to allow the fish docs to fully research these attacks, to facilitate their needs and keep them out of trouble. The Foundation's board held an emergency meeting; the directors want the science team to find out what this is, and then publish. They're betting on a major discovery here, and they want to take the credit. We're the only research team out here working on this; they want a big score."

Moss's frustration has now infected Malcolm Rafferty. "But what about people's lives? What about our lives? Do they understand we could be in serious danger here?"

"They're confident we can handle it, and with the way we've outfitted this ship, I agree, but let's hope it doesn't come to that. I feel the same as you, Razz; we've both seen enough battles."

Chapter 8

"Regal Duchess Cruises prides itself on offering unparalleled five-star service to our elite clientele. We're famous for offering only the highest level of premium service to our passengers traveling aboard our state-of-the-art ships under the motto: "Where every class is first class." Recently this has extended to every aspect of your cruising experience. Due to popular demand, Regal Duchess Cruises has now embarked on our all new RDC Green Campaign. That's right, RDC has gone green! Ask your cabin steward to schedule a green tour during your stay with us and be sure to ask about the option to offset the carbon footprint of your cruise by purchasing our available carbon credits program..."

"Honey? *Cathy?* Turn that thing off, will ya? Please?" A man emerges from the walk-in closet of his suite as he fights with the bowtie of his tuxedo.

"Ok, ok, It's off..." his wife Cathy answers as she grabs the remote and clicks off the TV.

Her husband stops in front of a mirror, still wrestling with his tie. "For some reason I can't stand that woman's voice; it grates on me."

"I only had it on because I was hoping they'd show some more tour information," she calmly answers as she applies her mascara. "We arrive in the Philippines tomorrow. I saw an article in Conde Nast Traveler; these islands are gorgeous. Did you know the Philippine archipelago has over seven thousand islands in it? And only two thousand are inhabited? Did you know they filmed the movie *Apocalypse Now* here?

"No, as a matter of fact I didn't," he answers cheerfully, "but I'm not surprised." He finally manages to get his bowtie neatly straightened. "Seven thousand islands, huh? Wow, that's a lot!"

With her makeup completed, Cathy turns to get up, but as she does, her long beaded gown swipes against the rattan chair she was seated on. "Oh crap!" she snaps, as she looks down to see some of the beading has been pulled out.

Her husband sees her distress. "Honey, don't worry, nobody will notice; you look fabulous, as always. So how do I look in this monkey suit?" He leans against the wall seductively, sliding a hand into his jacket pocket. "Yes, I'd like that martini shaken…"

"Ha ha, not bad… Well, I guess that makes me your femme-fatale then?"

"You got that right, baby. Now let's get down to the ballroom; they have a live orchestra tonight!" He steps smoothly toward his wife, takes her hand, pulls her close, then dips her gracefully…

Cathy looks up into her husband's eyes. "Martin! You're sure in a mood!"

Martin whispers to her softly, "The sea, the salt air, a beautiful woman; what more can a man ask for?" He then swings Cathy back on her feet.

She looks at her husband quizzically. "How long did you practice that corny line?"

Martin smiles. "Quite a while, actually. How'd I do?"

Down in the ballroom the party is in full swing as Martin and Cathy arrive via a glass elevator. "I'm not happy with the way this car is riding," Martin observes. "I'm going to speak to maintenance."

Cathy rolls her eyes. "Oh Martin, you haven't serviced elevators in years!"

"Once a mechanic always a mechanic. Anyway, a ship like this? I would love to get a closer look at how they mounted this shaft."

Cathy turns and looks into her husband's eyes with a sultry stare. "Well maybe later you can show me how your shaft is mounted. What do ya say, baby?"

Martin's face turns red as the doors slide open and the couple is hit by the din of loud conversation and Cuban rumba. He gazes out at the formally dressed crowd. "Wow, is this place great?" Martin takes Cathy's hand as she steps from the elevator onto the Italian marble floor. They pause a moment, in awe of the opulence that surrounds them.

The couple now stand at the center of the ship's giant, sparkling atrium that spans the entire height of the ship. The cavernous space is accented with marble columns, polished chrome paneling, and life-sized crystal sculptures of mermaids and dolphins resting inside gold leaf-embellished shell niches. The sculptures are flanked by brightly colored, sparkling glass mosaics depicting coral reefs and sea life.

Cathy looks lovingly at her husband. "Ok dear, you promised a fantastic second honeymoon, and you have certainly delivered!" Martin winks at Cathy, then spins her onto the dance floor where they're soon swallowed by a sea of tuxedos and evening gowns.

As the elegant dinner and dancing party goes into full swing on the upper decks, far below, in the deepest bowels of the ship, a group of men are hard at work. They are the lowest class, lowest paid of the crew on board. The sort that paying guests will never see, doing the work no one else is willing to do. On this night, they're on garbage duty.

The luxury cruise liner is four days out of Hong Kong and well outside territorial waters. The refuse hold is nearly full; it needs to be cleared. The men work on the bottom aft deck, dragging rotting garbage from a massive compartment using long rakes. Pulling large clumps of trash from the hold, they use the rakes to shove the trash down an angled platform into the sea. As the churning froth of the ship's screws leaves a silky silver path in the moonlight, the subtle illumination reveals a trail of refuse drifting off into the night.

One of the men is pushing a load of garbage down to the edge of the ramp when something suddenly hooks onto his rake, yanking both the rake and the man holding it overboard. So immediate was the event that none of the other men heard anything. Only one of the work crew caught a glimpse of what happened. In distress, he calls to the others, shouting that a man has just gone into the sea. They all rush to the edge of the ramp to peer down into the torrent below, straining for any sign of their shipmate.

The powerful screws of the ship's engines drone on as one of the work crew runs to alert the bridge that a man has gone overboard. The rest of the group stand silently, hoping for any sign of the missing man, but all know the slim chance for recovery has already passed. Most of the others go back to work; there is nothing they can do. If the officers come down and see they're not doing their jobs, they could lose them.

One man remains at the railing; he continues to peer over the edge. Straining for a better view, searching the darkness, suddenly he detects motion. His instincts tell him to pull back as his senses perceive the danger, but it's too late. The last thing he sees is the flash of white teeth inside huge jaws. The men nearby are knocked off their feet as the massive body of a tiger shark plows into them. She lands on the rear of the platform, the head and upper shoulders of the crewmen now clamped firmly inside her mouth.

She begins to thrash, violently shaking her head as the man's body is tossed from side to side. Gnashing into her victim's flesh, her teeth savagely saw through the man's upper torso until the lower half of his body finally breaks free. Blood sprays across the deck as terrified crewmen are sucked into the hellish scene. The shark continues to thrash, causing the flowing blood of the dead man to coat the deck, mixing with the ooze of garbage and creating a slimy putrid surface. The men scramble; they struggle to escape, but they are unable to get to their feet and unable to flee their attacker.

On the upper decks there is no sign of danger as the party guests are being seated for dinner in the main ballroom. Martin and Cathy sit side by side at a large round table for eight. Cathy is chatting with a couple from the Netherlands seated on her left. They introduce themselves as Pieter and Tineke. Martin is seated next to an insurance broker from Omaha, Nebraska, who is regaling him with the time the oracle himself, Warren Buffett, spoke at a meeting of his Rotary Club.

Martin nods politely, and, while looking over the menu, he nudges Cathy. "Hey, did you see this? They're featuring Asian delicacies tonight. Look at this stuff, I've never heard of any of this before. Look here, it says they have soup made out of shark fin!"

Cathy laughs. "No thanks, I'm having the filet minion and lobster tail. This Midwest girl is going surf & turf all the way." Cathy then turns to Pieter and Tineke. "So what are you two thinking of having?"

Pieter smiles. "I will have the steak as well. I think Tineke is having the grilled sea bass fillets."

Their waiter arrives to take the table's orders using an electronic touch pad. The group's selections are sent immediately back to the ship's enormous kitchen where a staff of one hundred is running on all cylinders. Waitstaff whisk trays of food out from the kitchen's swinging doors, while more enter the kitchen to pick up theirs. Inside, an army of line cooks working the stations are flying through their orders, assembling chic-looking gourmet plates by the dozen in a factory-like atmosphere of mechanized precision—all in an effort to create the illusion of personal service.

On the bridge, the ship's captain has just been informed of the man overboard. He cuts engines, then sends crewmen out with searchlights to scan the seas for any sign of the lost man. Then another call comes up from below, a report that some sort of disturbance is taking place on the lower aft deck. "It's probably another damn fight," the captain fumes. He turns to his first officer: "Send security down there to break it up. Use the Tasers if need be."

Down in the security office, a team of three men quickly assemble their gear. Each grabs a helmet and a utility belt containing a night stick, Taser, and nylon cuffs. As the security team makes their way down toward the lower aft deck, they radio up to the bridge to report that they're on their way. To avoid disturbing the guests, the team takes the stairs down three flights to the crew deck. After reaching the service level where guests are not allowed, they break into a full run, pounding down the corridor that leads to the area where the men on garbage duty are supposed to be working.

Bursting through an exterior hatchway, the three-man security detail runs out into the open night air, onto the aft deck, and straight into a horribly gruesome scene, as the ramp where the garbage crew were working is now littered with their savagely dismembered bodies.

The first security officer to arrive trips over a crewmen's butchered leg. Falling forward, he lands in a mass of blood, garbage, and snapping jaws as three zombie sharks instantly attack him. One bites down on the man's head, while the other two rage in a gruesome tug of war, ripping the man's body apart so quickly the other two members of the security team hardly have time to comprehend what they have just witnessed.

The two remaining security officers immediately attempt to run. In the process, one grabs for his radio, while the other reaches for the handle to the exterior hatch. As the two men attempt to flee, however, dozens more zombie sharks have appeared. The man who went for the door struggles to hold on to it, but he can't get to his feet. As his grip on the door handle slips away, he suddenly cries out in agony. He looks down to see the mutilated corpse of a dead shark biting into his thigh, pulling him away from the door. He reaches for his Taser, aims, then fires a high-voltage burst.

The shock from the Taser passes instantly through the body of the shark, then into his own. The security officer again shrieks in pain, but the Taser worked; the zombie shark suddenly lets go, as the now de-animated zombie shark drops to the deck in a heap of rotted flesh. Scrambling to his feet, the man is disoriented; he's also bleeding heavily, but he manages to get through the door on pure adrenaline. As he flees down the hallway, the cries of his partner fade behind him.

Chapter 9

In the deep ocean depths beneath the cruise liner, the zombie sharks gather. They mass in a relentless horde, drawn and driven by the energy field emanating from the talisman that has locked itself inside the jaws of the female tiger shark. As the horde grows, a vicious torrent of hundreds has now become thousands as it expands exponentially beyond the numbers the science team originally discovered. As the horde builds, the energy field driving them becomes more powerful, circulating, regenerating, flowing from the talisman carried by the tiger shark, into her horde, then back. With each cycle, the energy radiates outward at an even higher level, as it awakens and gathers every dead shark in the region, building until it explodes into an attack, an attack that must have a target.

The hoard's numbers have now reached a critical level. It's combustive energy suddenly sends it rocketing upwards in unison. The exponential mass of the surging horde powers an upwelling from the deep ocean. As the force generated by thousands of rapidly accelerating bodies causes the surface above them to balloon. The ocean explodes just off the stern of the cruise ship, opening wide a giant maw, as if the sea itself were vomiting this putrid horde. Thousands of zombie sharks flow out from the depths, hitting the stern of the cruise ship, then continuing on, sweeping forward in the form of an overwhelming wave of reanimated rotting shark flesh.

On the bridge, command officers look at each other with shared anxiety as they feel their ship inexplicably shudder. The subtle movement is followed by confusion as they are instantly inundated with emergency calls claiming the ship is under some sort of attack. The bridge crew's confusion turns to shock as the lone surviving security officer bursts onto the bridge in an adrenaline-fueled panic. Soaked in his own blood, he shouts to the captain that the ship is in extreme danger, that it's being overtaken by sharks.

"You've got to send power back to the engines, sir!" The security officer shouts. "We have to get away from here now!"

The captain is angered by the man's outburst. "What are you talking about? How can a ship this size be attacked by sharks? This is impossible!"

Then the first officer moves in. He sees the man's bleeding leg, and hears the calls now coming in from panicked crew. He turns to the captain, "We should send out a ship-wide emergency call, sir. I suggest we get the guests into their cabins for safety until we figure out what's going on."

The captain nods. "I agree. Put out a ship-wide call for all guests to return to their cabins, but just tell them it's a security alert, nothing more. It's too soon for a distress call. We don't even know what's happening; we are still fully operational. We don't want to risk instigating a panic."

In the ballroom, dinner has arrived with much fanfare as a fleet of waitstaff stand in unison behind each of the diners around

Martin and Cathy's table. With well-rehearsed flare, they simultaneously lift the silver covers to reveal the beautiful plates the kitchen has prepared. Cathy and Martin join the group in light applause. Then Pieter stands for a traditional Dutch toast: "Prost!" Everyone is raising their glasses when an alarm sounds, rudely interrupting the festive atmosphere. The alarm is followed by a ship-wide announcement:

"Ladies and gentlemen your attention please; we are currently experiencing a ship-wide security alert. Please return to your cabins immediately. We apologize for any inconvenience… to all guests, this is a ship-wide security alert. Please return to your cabins immediately…"

Cathy, Martin, and their fellow diners all look at each other as if one amongst them perhaps has some knowledge they can inject into the situation. "Security alert?" the insurance broker from Omaha repeats angrily. "But our dinner has just arrived!"

At that moment, the distant wail of muffled screams briefly fills the chasm of the atrium. For the vast majority of the party guests, however, the true nature of the sound fails to register. Martin looks at Cathy, who turns to see the frightened faces of the Dutch couple. She looks back again at Martin. "Let's go," she says calmly. "Something tells me we need to get out of here right now."

The group begins to leave. They push away their untouched plates as they gather phones, cameras, and handbags. They start to make their way back to their cabins. A large crowd is already heading for the glass elevators and a double set of escalators, but the insurance broker remains seated. He greedily cuts into his lobster tail, then quickly takes a bite from his steak. "You guys can go; I'm not leaving this behind. You know how much this stuff costs?"

Martin and Cathy suddenly find themselves jammed into a mass of confused, formally dressed cruise guests all looking for a way out at the same time. Many have gathered around the twin glass elevators, creating a choke point. Martin turns to Cathy and the Dutch couple. "I know another way," he directs. "Follow me; let's go."

They grab each other by the hand as Martin leads the group in the opposite direction, threading their way back through the crowd toward the kitchen. As they push their way through the kitchen's swinging doors, they are confronted by surprised staff who all look up, then begin shouting and pointing, as they try to tell these stupid tourists they've gone the wrong way, but Martin ignores them. Gripping Cathy's hand tightly, he marches the group through the kitchen.

Martin pushes past distraught line cooks, waiters, and cleaning staff until he locates the service elevator on the far side of the room. He quickly assesses the elevator's control pad. "We'll need a keycard to access this one," Martin observes as he puts his arm out to stop a passing waiter. "Excuse me sir," he quips sarcastically, then grabs the card clipped to the stunned man's jacket. Martin swipes the keycard across the elevator's sensor, triggering the doors to slide open as the two couples hurry inside. Cathy kisses Martin's cheek as the doors close behind them.

"Ok folks," Martin says politely, "now that we have that mess behind us, what deck level are you and Tineke on, Pieter?"

Pieter laughs. "Martin, that was impressive! We are on deck three, but I must admit, Tineke and I were quite frightened out there with all of those people."

"Oh yes!" adds Tineke excitedly. "I felt like we were in a movie!"

Down in the ballroom, the crowd grows increasingly agitated as the overloaded elevators become even more bogged down. A few staff members are attempting to direct the crowd toward other exits, but nobody is paying attention. The escalators nearby are also overwhelmed as a throng of guests push their way onto them. Then the atrium once again echoes with a rising swell of muffled cries that appear to be coming from the rear of the ship.

A rumble of excited chatter flows through the crowd as people begin shoving and pushing to get onto the escalators. The room fills again with screams, this time much louder, alerting the crowd that whatever is causing them is getting closer. A wave of fear riffles through the crowd of five hundred people attempting to exit through narrow gaps at the same time.

* * *

The service elevator's electronic voice announces the arrival on deck three. "Wow, thanks so much!" exclaims Pieter. "Your service is better than Regal Duchess!"

"All in a day's work for my elevator genius," adds Cathy. "We're just the next deck up. Would you two like to meet for breakfast tomorrow?"

Tineke looks at Pieter. "That sounds great!"

"Absolutely!" adds Pieter. "How about nine then?"

Just then the doors of the service elevator slide open, and the two couples are instantly hit by a cacophony of shouting and screaming. "Oh my! What is that!" Tineke shouts.

Martin looks quickly outside into the corridor then jumps back inside. "Holy mother of Jesus!" he shouts. "There're sharks out there!" He rushes to close the doors again.

"Martin, what's going on?" Cathy screams. "Did you say sharks?"

"Sharks!" Martin shouts as he pounds the button. "The whole place is full of sharks!"

The elevator is slow to respond, but finally the doors begin to slide shut as the frightened group inside watch other guests run past the opening. The doors are halfway closed when a reanimated dead shark suddenly comes into view, fiercely biting and snapping. Its jaws lash into the leg of a passing man, knocking him to the floor just in front of them. "Help me!" the man shouts. He grabs hold of the closing door, signaling it to stop and automatically open again. Martin and Pieter grab the man's hand and try to pull him inside. As he cries out for the last time, the man looks up at Martin as blood gushes from his mouth. His hands go limp as he is pulled from the edge of the doorway and disappears from view.

"My god Martin, get these doors shut!" Cathy shouts.

"They're closing! They're closing!" screams Martin as Tineke sinks to the floor, crying.

The doors begin to close again, and through the opening, the two couples can clearly see what look like dead, decomposed sharks, moving at incomprehensibly frightening speed.

Suddenly the sharks turn toward the opening. One begins rabidly biting the edge of the steel door, triggering an automatic reversal that signals the doors to open once more. Martin madly pounds the button again, as Pieter kicks at the shark's nose, trying to dislodge its jaws from the door. Two more sharks join in as they try to force their way through the door. Pieter and now Cathy kick at them furiously as they shout and plead for the doors to close. The doors are nearly closed when one of the sharks lunges at Pieter. The upper half of the shark's body enters the elevator just as the doors close around it.

This time Martin is ready; he slams the emergency stop button, causing the elevator to shut down, cutting the power to the doors and halting them mid-cycle. The zombie shark is now trapped between the two doors. It thrashes against them as it tries to free itself, its jaws snapping as it begins to force its way through the opening, pushing the doors apart with its body and making its way inside the elevator compartment.

"Pieter!" Martin shouts. "Quick, give me a leg up!"

Cathy steps out of the way, as Pieter kneels down. Martin then places his foot on Pieter's knee, reaches toward the metal ceiling panels, and knocks one to the floor.

"I need some help here!" Martin pleads as he lifts the stiff sheet metal above his head, then plunges the corner of it down into the shark. Pieter grabs one side of the panel as he and Martin ram the sharp corner down into the shark again. With each strike, they cut deeper into the zombie shark's rotted flesh until they finally sever the shark's head. Pieter then kicks the shark's body out through the opening as Martin releases the stop button. The doors reactivate, then finally close, leaving the lifeless head of a zombie shark staring up at them from the floor of the elevator.

"Martin, your hands, you're bleeding!" Cathy pulls a tissue from her purse in an attempt to stop the flow of blood.

"Honey, it's ok, I'm fine. It's a small cut is all."

Pieter has gone to comfort his wife, who is sitting in the corner, he's holding her and doing his best to keep her from looking at the severed head of the shark lying on the floor. Cathy, seeing how upset they both are, unties the silk evening wrap from her shoulders, folds it in half, and then drapes it over the head.

Pieter looks up at Cathy from the floor. "Thank you."

"Oh it's no big deal," Cathy smiles. "I was raised on a farm. Besides, that thing really stinks!"

Martin looks over at Pieter. "We're not safe like this, but I have an idea."

Chapter 10

On the bridge of the stricken cruise liner, the captain receives the grim confirmation that the ship is indeed under lethal attack as he and the other officers watch a security camera feed.

"My god," the captain whispers, looking on in shock as passengers are overwhelmed by a rapid onslaught of savagely attacking sharks. "I've been at sea for twenty-eight years, and this is how it ends… this is lunacy…"

"This is impossible," observes the first officer. "How can this be happening? Sharks? On board? This is completely crazy!"

The captain's face is sternly resolved as he turns to his senior bridge crew. "Send out an emergency distress call immediately. Call down to security, tell them they have free rein to use whatever weapons and means necessary to try to neutralize the situation. Call the medical officer, tell him to expect casualties, and send out another ship-wide announcement. I want all passengers to seek shelter. Tell them we have confirmed intruders on board. I want all non-essential crew to stay in their quarters until further notice. This means now, people! Let's get on it!" Then the captain pauses.

"You sir," the captain commands, as he points at the security officer still standing in front of him. "Get down to medical. You're bleeding all over my bridge."

* * *

The leading edge of the zombie horde enters the ship's cavernous central atrium, yet the reanimated sharks go unnoticed by the vast majority of the crowd as they push, shove, and struggle to cram themselves onto the escalators and into the twin glass elevators. The zombie sharks glide effortlessly across the marble floor, their mutilated and putrefied bodies still possessing the grace and agility that was once their birthright as apex predators, their reanimated corpses now propelled by the unseen energy field that surrounds them.

On the far side of the room, near the edge of the crowd gathered at the base of the escalators, the insurance broker from Omaha is still seated. Having devoured his steak and lobster, he then reaches for a steaming bowl of soup sitting nearby that was left behind by one of the other guests at the table. He's been watching the mayhem taking place in front of him for the past fifteen minutes. All the while he's been congratulating himself, laughing at the stupidity of these people.

He's an expert in his field, after all; he knows the actuarial tables inside and out. The weather conditions are excellent, he can tell the ship is not sinking, they haven't grounded, and the fire alarms have not gone off, which tells him the odds that a serious emergency is really taking place are in fact minuscule. Especially aboard a ship this size. He dips a spoon into the soup, raising up from the yellowish opaque broth, glistening white strands of gelatinous shark fin. He slurps it into his mouth. "Mmmmm! Not bad!" he announces. "I can see why people pay big money for this!" At that moment, unnoticed by the insurance broker from Omaha, an eight-foot-long zombie bull shark is rocketing across the atrium's floor on a targeted path straight for him. The bull shark rams the chair the man is sitting on, and the impact knocks him to the floor. Startled and disoriented, the insurance broker has no idea what has just happened until he sees a very large shark pass just inches away.

He reaches up to grab the edge of the table, but in his panic only manages to grasp the tablecloth. As plates and glassware crash to the floor, the bull shark whips back, its jaws open. It is ready to strike, yet the insurance broker can't believe what he is seeing; it's clearly impossible. At that moment the shark's powerful jaws sink into the man's full stomach. With the bull shark now locked onto its victim, the long-dead zombie thrashes violently, slashing open the man's abdomen as his howling cries fill the cavernous room.

Two hammerhead sharks join the attack; simultaneously they tear into the man's legs and shred his body to bits. The zombie sharks attack as if in a feeding frenzy, as if fulfilling a drive to consume flesh even though the reanimated dead sharks no longer have the ability to feed; only the instinct to kill remains.

The shrill cries of the dying man catch the attention of the agitated crowd. The formally dressed guests surrounding the escalators and the glass elevators all turn to see what is happening. The full scope of their situation becomes clear as they see hundreds of sharks pouring into the atrium from the corridor that leads to the pool area.

A brief moment of shared initial shock and disbelief quickly vaporizes as individuals within the group begin to perceive the overwhelming danger, and uncontrolled fear takes them all in its grip. No longer thinking for themselves, their minds are now driven by the most primitive part of their brains as the areas of higher reasoning shut down. A numbness takes over, a feeling as if the individual is in a dream, as if they are viewing what is happening to them from someplace else. Cut off from reason, they rapidly lose the ability to control their actions; this is what fear does to the mind, this is how minds become a mob.

A crescendo of screams rises from the heaving tracks of the escalators and the people packed onto them are suddenly pinned in even more tightly. The pressure causes some to spill over the railings and onto the floor below as the crush of bodies surges forward. The desperate begin climbing over each other, grabbing and clawing at the hair, clothing, and flesh of the people beneath them. But the reanimated dead sharks are too fast for even the strongest of them, as the zombie horde overwhelms the human mob.

The last group to cram themselves inside one of the glass elevators looks on in horror at the deadly, blood-soaked riot now exploding in front of them. Terrorized faces outside press up tightly against the elegant glass as the lucky few inside slowly rise up from the floor. The people left behind on the outside frantically pound on the glass as the zombie sharks attack, sending a spray of blood shooting up in front of the passengers inside.

The glass capsule reverberates with the startled cries of its passengers. The occupants at the front of the car try to turn away, pushing to the rear. They see all too clearly the people they were just standing next to are now being violently killed. Yet some find they cannot look away; as if in a trance, their gaze remains fixed silently downward toward the slaughter now taking place on the atrium floor.

Like a fast-moving river far above flood stage, the zombie horde sweeps up over the escalators and crashes onto the terrified people beneath, mincing and shredding the panicked mob as hundreds of reanimated shark bodies tear apart those of their victims. The group inside the over-packed glass elevator struggles to find room to breathe. Pushing against the outer walls, they lean against the control panel, lighting up all of the numbered buttons. Nobody knows where the car is going, or on what floor it will stop, they only know that they have escaped.

The terrified screams and cries emanating from the crowd below are steadily squelched as the zombie horde reaches the top of the escalators. The occupants of the elevator look on as the last of the living beneath them are snuffed out. Then, like a brushfire that has consumed its fuel, the horde recedes back to the main floor of the atrium where it circles briefly before flowing on rapidly toward the ship's massive kitchen.

Meanwhile, inside the elevator, a ship-wide alert broadcasts over the car's speakers. Individuals begin arguing for the group to shut up so they can hear what is being announced… "We repeat, this is a ship-wide emergency alert. Dangerous intruders are on board; please seek shelter in a secure area immediately… this is a ship-wide emergency alert, please seek shelter immediately…"

At that moment the elevator's cheerful pre-programmed electronic voice cuts in, announcing the elevator's arrival on deck seven: "Please watch your step as you exit. Have a nice day, and thank you for choosing Regal Duchess Cruise Line…" The polished chrome rear doors slide open to reveal deck seven is a raging flood of zombie sharks. Frantic shouting interrupts as passengers begin fighting with each other. Several attempt to hit the control buttons at the same time, as they scream for the doors to close again.

A few inside the elevator attempt to escape into the corridor, only to be instantly set upon by a group of long-dead zombie gray reef sharks who viciously tear apart the fleeing passengers. The zombie sharks then turn their attention toward the remaining people now trapped inside the glass elevator. With nothing to hold them back, the zombie sharks race through the open doors straight into human flesh, coating the glass walls with blood as they tear the shrieking occupants to pieces.

Chapter 11

Martin stands in front of the control panel of the service elevator, his mind racing. As Cathy looks on, he knows he must act quickly. He's certain the heavy steel structure will withstand the attack, but only if the elevator is isolated between floors. The mood inside the small compartment that has now become their lifeboat is tense as Martin turns to his wife.

"We're on deck three. We need to be in-between floors if we're going to survive. I'm going to send us up to deck two, then hit the stop button again before we get there. This will shut it down and prevent anyone from calling this elevator, and it will keep the doors from opening again."

"Do it now! Please!" pleads Pieter as he holds Tineke closely.

Martin looks at Cathy, who quickly nods reassuringly. Martin swallows hard, then presses the button for deck two. As the elevator begins moving, Martin counts the seconds, then mashes the stop button, cutting the power and halting the car mid-cycle.

"What do we do now?" asks Pieter,

"We need to check and make sure we're actually positioned in between the floors," Martin replies.

"How do we do that?"

"I've got to push the doors open and have a look,"

"Honey, is that a good idea?" Cathy questions. "We don't know what's out there!"

"It's the only way to know for sure; these doors are only closed, they aren't locked. Something can still push through like before." Martin then turns to face the two doors. Grabbing one side, he then places the heel of his hand against the opposite door, straining against the sluggish gears of the deactivated motor. In response, the doors move slightly. He tries to peer through the tiny opening, but it's not wide enough.

"Can you see anything?" asks Pieter

"No, the opening's too small," Martin complains, he leans in again, pushing harder against the doors until they open farther, and a slim shaft of light from the floor above fills the compartment. Martin sighs in disgust. The opening is positioned at the upper quarter of the door. He looks up at the light shining down on them. "We need to go back down a bit. What we're looking at up there is deck two…" At that moment a zombie black tip shark bursts through the narrow opening, its madly snapping jaws just inches from Martin's face, as its head thrashes against the elevator doors.

"Martin! Look out, oh my god!" Cathy screams,

Martin grabs the metal ceiling panel. "Pieter, quick! Help me put this over the opening!"

The two men shove the panel up against the nose of the crazed zombie shark. In unison they begin pounding with their fists, trying to force the shark back out, but now a second black tip zombie shark has joined in the attack.

"They're too strong!" Pieter shouts. "They're going to get through!"

"The escape hatch," Martin shouts as he glances at Pieter. "Just above this ceiling panel we took down is the escape hatch; every elevator has one. Quick, I'll hold them back; you get the girls out."

"But what about you?"

"I'll be fine, just be ready to pull me up when I let go."

Pieter turns to see Cathy ripping away the lower half of her beaded evening gown with a metal nail file from her purse. Kicking off her high heels, she looks at Pieter. "Ok, give me a boost." Pieter grabs her by the waist, holding her up as she scrambles to place a knee on his shoulder. She reaches for the hatch, grabs the handle, turns it, then shoves it open. Martin is struggling to hold back the two zombie sharks. Their jaws snap savagely, their teeth loudly scraping against the sheet metal, as they try to force their way through the opening.

"Better make it quick guys!"

Pieter pushes Cathy up through the opening then grabs Tineke by the hand. "I'm scared!" she sobs in Dutch.

"It's ok darling. It's going to be ok," he says reassuringly as he lifts her up through the hatch. Cathy then grabs her, helping her to get through the small opening. For Pieter's turn, he balances one foot on the hand railing that runs across the rear wall, then, grabbing Cathy's outstretched hand, pulls himself up high enough to grab the edge of the hatch. Breathing heavily, he squeezes his tall frame up and out of the compartment. With Cathy holding his legs, Pieter then lowers his head and right shoulder back down through the opening,

"Martin!" Pieter shouts. "We're ready! Run now!"

Martin turns to see Pieter's outstretched hand just a few feet away. *No time to think about this...* Martin then gives the panel one last hard shove, pushing away from the wall as he spins, then takes a large stride as he lunges toward the railing. He grabs Pieter's arm, then manages to get a grip with his left hand on the edge of the hatch opening. As Martin struggles to get up through the hatch he suddenly sees Pieter's expression change, shifting in a flash from joy to horror.

"Don't look down!" Pieter shouts. "Just let me pull you up!"

It's at that moment that Martin suddenly realizes something is wrong, that he is in incredible pain. He looks down to see a five-foot-long zombie shark has latched onto his left foot. The shark's body now dangles from the floor; the added weight prevents Martin from pulling himself up through the hatch. In spite of the agonizing pain, Martin begins kicking at the nose of the shark, jamming his heel down as hard as he can. With each kick, the searing pain shoots through his body like a high-voltage jolt.

Pieter, with Cathy's help, is slowly pulling Martin higher up into the hatch. The zombie shark is now swinging above the floor as it ferociously shakes its head. Its white dead eyes flash in the dim light, its finless rotting corpse filling the compartment with a horrible stench as its teeth tear into Martin's flesh.

A second shark suddenly forces its way through the opening and is propelled across the compartment, heading straight for Martin's other leg but misses it slightly. Instead, the second black tip strikes the shark hanging from Martin's foot, the impact sends both sharks to the floor. Pieter pulls Martin up through the opening. Cathy quickly closes the hatch. The two men then spontaneously begin sobbing, overwhelmed with emotion.

Cathy sees Martin's injury. "Martin! Your foot is bleeding badly!"

"Don't worry about me," Martin assures her, then he takes Cathy's hand, pulling her close. "We're ok, we're safe now, I promise."

* * *

Back on the bridge, the radio officer is in contact with the Philippine Coast Guard; he turns to the captain who stands just behind him: "They want to know the nature of the emergency, sir. What should I tell them?"

"Tell them the ship is currently under attack, and we're suffering severe casualties."

A few seconds later, after another exchange with the Coast Guard, the radio officer looks up at the captain. "Sir, they're asking if we have sharks on board."

The captain's initial shock vanishes quickly. "Affirmative. Tell whoever's on that line we've got people dying out here. We don't know how many sharks are on board, but based on reports from the crew, and our security cameras, there must be hundreds of them. Tell the Coast Guard they better send us everything they've got."

The officer relays the message, then turns once more to the captain. "They're on their way, sir. Emergency medical evacuation choppers in one hour, cutters in five."

* * *

As dawn breaks across the South China Sea, two long-range Coast Guard rescue helicopters approach the stricken vessel as she sits motionless on a calm, flat sea. The two flight crews radio back visual confirmation, then begin to chat amongst themselves on a separate channel. "That must be her," says one of the pilots. "The coordinates match up, but she looks pretty quiet from out here. I don't see any signs of damage, do you?"

"No," answers another, "but in the briefing they said to expect this…"

"She looks damn spooky to me…" adds another. "After what happened at that resort, I'm not looking forward to what we find down there."

* * *

Inside the dimly lit elevator shaft, on the grease and dust-covered roof of the car, Martin attempts to shift his weight, trying to find a more comfortable position in between the cables and the door motor, but the throbbing pain shooting up from his ankle is excruciating. "Fifteen years as a surgical nurse, I've never seen a wound like this," Cathy remarks as she cradles Martin's foot in her lap. "I think I have the bleeding under control. It's a good thing you don't wear clip-ons; your black tie made a perfect tourniquet." She gently pulls away a corner of the makeshift bandage. "But you've got to keep this elevated; try not to move." Then she turns to Pieter. "How is Tineke doing?"

Pieter has his wife bundled inside his tuxedo jacket. "She keeps trying to speak, but I'm not sure what she is saying."

"It's the shock," Cathy answers confidently. "Keep her warm and just let her talk. As long as she's conscious, we're ok. And as for you," she gives Martin a sharp look, "quit wiggling around. You're going to start bleeding again. This is serious; I said keep this foot elevated and I meant it."

Martin smiles at Cathy. "Well, we're nine stories up from the bottom of the ship; I'd say that's pretty elevated."

"Ha ha, ok smart ass, if you're able to make corny jokes, I know you're going to be just fine."

Just then Tineke interrupts. She's speaking in Dutch, when Pieter breaks in: "Wait, Tineke says she hears something. We must be quiet a moment, please."

All four of them wait silently. At first they hear nothing, no more screams, no more sounds of running crowds of people, no alarms, nothing… then gradually they all begin to detect something. Cathy looks at Martin. "I hear helicopters."

Pieter's expression brightens as he looks down at Tineke. "Yes darling! You were right!"

Not long after the sounds of the helicopters fade, they hear voices coming from inside the elevator beneath them,

"Wow, what happened in here?"

"Looks like there was a fight; looks like the sharks might have lost this one," then someone begins pushing the doors open,

Martin tries to sit up when another voice breaks in, "At least this elevator's not like what we found on deck seven."

Martin looks over at Pieter: "Quick, open the hatch!"

Pieter moves within reach then opens the escape hatch. "Hey! Hello down there!" He leans over to see a man's face appear in the opening; he's wearing an RDC security uniform. The security officer becomes emotional as he looks up at Pieter: "Thank God, are you all right? Is anyone else up there?"

Chapter 12

It's early morning aboard *Fearless*. Moss has called an emergency meeting of all personnel: "Some of you are already aware there was another attack last night. I would appreciate it if all of you would ignore the sensationalism that's out there on the web, and most certainly do not contribute. We are a science vessel; I've been in contact with the Foundation directly. They don't want anyone from this ship using social media to communicate anything about these events to anyone. You all signed nondisclosures when you came on board; that certainly applies here. The board members consider any and all information we gather to be proprietary, and they have assured me the penalties for doing otherwise will be severe. Does everyone understand what I have just told you?" Nods of agreement...

"Ok then. For those of you who haven't heard, yes, there was another attack that took place on a cruise ship last night. The numbers are still coming in, but the coast guard tells me they believe as many as a thousand people were killed. As unbelievable as this may sound, we have highly credible reports from first responders that, along with the victims, they've been recovering shark remains all over the ship, on nearly every deck. The Coast Guard is sending one of their choppers over with specimens they'd like us to examine. The science team has a lab prepared; staff are standing by to receive this forensic evidence and report on what they find. Once again, the Philippine authorities have been grateful for our assistance; they're appreciative of the Foundation's cooperation, and for the participation by this crew. They've asked that I thank you directly.

"Many of you I've known personally for several years, and many of you have been with this ship since her launch. I don't need to tell you this latest event is a game changer. What we've learned in the past few days since these attacks began is that dry land doesn't stop them, and the interior of a cruise ship doesn't stop them. So anyone who wants out is not going to get any flack from me; I understand completely. Just let me know by the end of the day and we'll make arrangements to have you evacuated off this ship. That's everything we've got right now; as I learn anything further, you will all be the first to know.

As the crowd disperses, Falcon and Marsh rise slowly from their chairs; they look at each other with shared bewilderment.

"I don't even know how to begin wrapping my mind around this," says Marsh.

"Do you doubt anything Mr. Moss is reporting?" asks Falcon.

"Not at all; he's one of the most solidly reasonable men I've ever known, and that fact alone has me extremely worried. Whatever we're facing here, Tom, I'm absolutely certain it's a phenomenon previously unknown, but I'm concerned we may be getting in over our heads on this one."

"I agree," adds Falcon, "but the specimens they recovered from the cruise ship are on their way. I suggest we focus on the science."

"True, old friend, you're absolutely correct. Performing necropsies on dead sharks will be the most normal thing we've done since this nightmare began. I'm actually looking forward to seeing the specimens; they're our first viable opportunity to begin finding some answers."

* * *

Rafferty enters the bridge and finds Moss standing alone, his hands on his hips as he stares out blankly across the empty bay they're anchored in and the open sea beyond it.

"Do you have a plan?"

"Not yet, but I'm working on it."

Moss turns, he looks Rafferty directly in the eye, "You and I have seen a lot of shit together, Razz, but for every mission we went on, we went in prepared; we had intelligence, we had air support, we had an extraction team on standby, we had a massive military structure behind us."

"And we were younger; don't forget that one."

"Yeah, that too," Moss pauses, "but this time we have none of those things. It's just us, and frankly, I'm wishing I had picked up on what you were trying to tell me two days ago, when we still had the chance to get this ship the hell out of here, and I want you to know I'm sorry for that; I should have listened to you."

"Ax, whatever you decide to do we're with you a hundred percent, myself included. We can't start second guessing ourselves. We need to move forward; we've got to be ready to act."

Later that afternoon Marsh and Falcon are in the lab when they hear the sound of a chopper as it approaches the helipad. "We're up," quips Marsh excitedly, as he looks toward Falcon, who is already heading for the door. Falcon pauses at the doorway, and looks back at Marsh. "Let's go see what Santa brought us."

The chopper is just lifting off again as the two scientists step onto the helipad. Two crew members are walking toward them, each carrying one end of an overstuffed body bag. "Did you guys order the dead fish? Well here you go!" They drop the heavily loaded bag at the feet of Marsh and Falcon, then walk away.

Marsh starts to lift one end of the body bag. "Shit, that's heavy!"

"Come on you lightweight, be a man!" Falcon gibes. "We're field researchers; we're the commandos of the scientific world."

The lab door bursts open as Marsh, Falcon, and their two graduate student assistants, Brian and Alistair, haul the heavy black nylon bag inside, then heave it up onto a stainless steel table. Marsh then looks across the table at Falcon. "Grab your gloves and goggles, gentlemen; let's get started."

Falcon and the two assistants look on as Marsh reaches up to the top of the bag and takes hold of the heavy waterproof zipper. Slowly drawing it down, he opens the bag. "Oh god that's a bad smell!" Falcon exclaims and recoils as he reflexively reaches behind him for a box of surgical masks.

"I'll take one of those," adds Marsh,

"Me too!" says Alistair

"Hey mate," pleads Brian, "hand me one as well, will you?"

Marsh pulls back the sides of the body bag, revealing the remains of four quite ordinary-looking, mid-sized sharks all lying belly up. It's obvious to Dr. Marsh that the specimens had been hurriedly stuffed into the bag like oversized sardines. "Well this is certainly interesting…"

Falcon leans in to have a look. "Yes indeed, these guys look pretty puny to be dangerous man-eaters, much less guilty of attacking a cruise-liner."

Marsh and the two students open the bag further, but as they do, one of the corpses manages to slip off the top of the pile. Its decomposing body slams to the floor, the impact sends a splatter of rotted tissue squirting across Alistair's shirt.

"Oh dude, you got nailed!" Brian announces. He winces as Alistair wipes the stinking ooze from his chin.

"Thanks… thanks for that," Alistair answers. He then looks down at the slime splattered across his shirt and wipes away a glob of the stinking gelatinous goo with his gloved hand. "That's just gross…" he observes. "So Dr. Marsh, if this attack happened just last night, how can these specimens be so decomposed? I mean, look at the condition of this tissue." He holds up the residue, smearing the rotted yellowish slime between his fingers. "These sharks would need to be dead for nearly a week for this level of decay to set in, wouldn't you agree?"

"Yes Alistair I would," answers Marsh as he and Falcon both kneel down to the floor for a closer look. Marsh's intense scientific curiosity shields him from the grotesque physical state of the specimen. "Well hello, what's going on here?" Marsh runs a gloved hand down the jagged cut where the shark's dorsal fin once was.

"Look here, Peter," observes Falcon. "Both of the pectoral fins are also missing."

"All four of these sharks have had their fins cut off, Dr. Marsh," Alistair remarks as he and Brian examine the three sharks still inside the body bag,

"Well, from the looks of it," Brian adds, his arms elbow-deep inside the bag as he rummages through the corpses, "my first reaction would be to assume that whoever packed the bag did this, so they would all easily fit inside, but I look at these cuts and... well, they're old. They're all as decomposed as the bodies. It doesn't really make sense." Brian pauses, he stares down at Marsh and Falcon, who are kneeling beside the shark on the floor. "Is the Coast Guard certain these specimens were collected from the cruise ship? Because, to be honest, these sharks look like they were killed by a fin boat to me."

Falcon leaps to his feet, pulling the mask from his face as he grabs the corner of the table in order to steady himself. Marsh looks up at him. "What's wrong? You're looking pretty startled. Tom, are you all right?"

"I'll be fine; I'm just going out for some air. Is that all right with you?"

"Of course," Marsh answers. He stands and looks at his friend. "I'll bring you up to speed when you get back. We're going to start dissecting these specimens so we can collect samples for analysis."

Falcon rips the gloves from his hands, removes his goggles, then walks outside into the blinding afternoon sun. He goes to the railing, gripping it tightly as a dizzying numbness washes over him. His mind is spinning and it's hard to breathe; he feels his chest closing in as if a giant weight had just been placed there... *Oh dear god what have I done? What have I done?*

Paralyzing guilt overwhelms him as all of the pieces begin drawing together, and the total picture becomes clear: the night dive down to the kill-zone, the talisman, the video image of the tiger shark. *It was her... The shaman was right, somehow he knew... The power of the talisman must have spread throughout the kill field... but how can this be possible?* Then the words of the old shaman on the beach begin to echo in Falcon's head: *"I know who you are and what you have done..."* And now, so does Dr. Thomas Falcon.

Chapter 13

Moss, Rafferty, and four crew members are on the bridge, looking at a large chart Moss has spread out on a table, when Falcon walks in. Moss looks up. "Dr. Falcon," the chief asks, his imposing frame dominating even those of the hardened veteran solders gathered around him. "What can I do for you?"

"It was me…" The words suddenly appear as if spoken by someone else, and there's no retracting them, there's no going back to the moment before the words left his mouth. The only way from here is forward. Falcon's path now lies in front of him; he can see it clearly. The old shaman was right; it will be a difficult and painful path, but Falcon knows he has no choice: he must follow it. At that very moment, the fear that had consumed him vanishes and is replaced by a focused beam of conscious clarity. Falcon looks Moss directly in the eye: "The unauthorized dive, the empty tank; it was me."

Moss looks at Rafferty, who then turns to the other men. "Can you excuse us for a few minutes, gentlemen?" The four crew members turn to leave; each one gives Falcon an intimidating look of disgust as he walks past.

Rafferty then takes a step back behind the table as Moss moves forward, keeping his focus on Falcon. "You have my attention, sir," says Moss. "I'm listening."

Falcon's gaze doesn't waver; his eyes remain locked on Moss. "This is going to sound crazy, perhaps..."

"After what I've seen the past few days?" answers Moss. "I seriously doubt that anything you say will shock me, Dr. Falcon."

"All of this, everything that's been happening, these mass shark attacks, it's all because of something I did. All of this is because of my ignorance; this is all my fault."

Moss leans back against the table and sighs. He then folds his arms in front of him as his expression softens. "You're telling me you believe all of these horrific attacks, made by thousands of sharks, were triggered by you alone? By something you did? How is this possible? I don't understand what you're really trying to tell me here. Let's go back a step; you said you were the one who made the unauthorized dive last week. Why don't we start there."

Falcon relaxes slightly. "I came on board to work with a colleague I respect very highly. A man whom I, and many others, consider to be one of the best scientific minds in our field of study, and I let him down. I allowed emotion to cloud my judgment, and I acted impulsively on that emotion. That day, when we dove on that kill-zone, and I saw all of those hundreds of mutilated sharks, I was overwhelmed and filled with rage. I wanted to gain control of my emotional state. Also, I now realize I selfishly sought revenge against those that perpetrated this senseless mass killing. So that night I took the tank and dive gear; I dove back down to the kill-zone, and I left something behind, something extremely powerful..."

"You just said you left something behind. What exactly do you mean by that? What did you leave behind, Dr. Falcon?"

"It was a Vodun talisman, what you may know as *Voodoo*. In this case, it was an object that has been in my family for many generations, an object that was brought from Africa by my ancestors. It had been passed to me by my grandmother in Jamaica. She had always told me it held great power, but I always believed this to be simply folklore, part of my culture. But that night, after what I had experienced seeing the kill-zone for the first time, I decided to use the talisman. It was meant to be ceremonial; it was meant only for me; I had intended for it to be a personal, private gesture. This is why I made the dive alone and in secret, but what I didn't know is that my grandmother was right; this talisman truly is extremely powerful."

As Rafferty stands nearby, he watches both men in silence; he observes and listens to every word, analyzing every movement and facial expression Falcon makes, searching for a signal, any sort of signal that might alert him to a deeper meaning, the truth hiding behind the words.

Moss is growing more agitated. He wants answers, yet what Falcon is giving him just creates more questions. "So you made an unauthorized, high-risk, solo night dive all so you could leave some Voodoo charm behind? I still don't see how this adds up to you being responsible for these mass attacks. The sharks we found down on the sea floor, they're all dead. They can't attack anybody. I'm giving you the benefit of the doubt, but you're still not making much sense, Dr. Falcon."

"It's called reanimation, Mr. Moss." Falcon's tone is reasoned as he moves closer to the table. His hands are at his sides, his palms facing outward toward Moss. "In Voodoo tradition, it's considered a dark art, a forbidden practice, whereby a deceased corpse is revived in order to do the bidding of its master. The corpse has not been brought back to life; it's just been animated like a puppet by the power of the talisman used to revive it. A power directed by the person controlling the talisman.

"Think of it as an amplifier; the talisman increases and intensifies the energy coming from whoever or whatever uses it. In this case, I placed the talisman inside the mouth of a tiger shark. As best I can decipher, the talisman reanimated her. She in turn reanimated the other sharks in the kill-zone. The talisman is controlling her, driving her like an engine, and the other sharks are all being driven by this same force. Call it an energy field; it must be drawing them in like a magnet. They're all following her."

Moss glances at Rafferty, then back at Falcon. "So you're saying that somehow this talisman you left down there inside a dead shark is powering these other sharks, and that it has *reanimated them*?"

"Yes, that's exactly what I'm saying." Falcon takes a step back as he places his hands on his hips. "I know it sounds crazy," he pauses, then raises his hands briefly to his face as if in prayer, "but a mass of sharks attacking a beach resort, or a cruise ship, is just as crazy and yet these two events have actually happened. When I placed the talisman inside the mouth of that tiger shark, I now realize that, unwittingly, I triggered the reanimation of that shark, and somehow through her, the rest of the dead as well. In Voodoo, these reanimated dead beings are called zombies. Mr. Moss, these aren't just sharks that are attacking people; these are reanimated zombie sharks."

Moss calmly rises from the table he was leaning against. "Well Dr. Falcon, I thank you for your candor in admitting it was you who made that dive, but other than that I'm not sure what to make of the rest of your story. Mr. Rafferty and I will certainly keep everything you've told us under consideration, and for now at least, let's keep this between us. I know Dr. Marsh is hard at work down in the lab. It would mean a lot to this crew, and the Foundation that is funding your stay here, if you can continue to assist him in making a significant scientific contribution. We need solutions, Dr. Falcon, actionable solid solutions. Do you understand what I'm telling you?"

"Yes, Mr. Moss, I understand you very clearly. I apologize for my disruption. If you need anything further from me, I'll be down in the lab."

Falcon walks to the door then closes it behind him as he leaves. Moss then turns to Rafferty. "What the fuck was that all about? This crap is going to push me off the edge, Razz."

"Holly shit, Ax, maybe we should check this guy for drugs, because that story makes me think he's been smoking something."

"Yeah, could be, but let's be serious here. What did you make of what he told you, Razz? I don't mean what he said, but what did he *tell* you?"

"He's telling the truth; at least he's telling what he believes to be true. I mean, jokes aside, this guy's no dummy, and yet he really thinks he somehow caused all of this."

"I agree, and frankly it has me pretty concerned. You want to know the worst part? My gut tells me he is connected somehow, and whatever is really happening here, it's long from over."

Chapter 14

Down in the lab, Marsh and Alistair have two of the specimens opened up, and are examining the contents of the sharks' stomachs and digestive tracts, while Brian has been carefully collecting tissue samples from the shark's teeth and mouths for genetic analysis. Falcon walks into the lab and confidently grabs his kit from the table as he prepares to assist.

"Tom, you're back, that's great!" Marsh looks up, smiling.

Falcon smiles. "Reporting for duty, sir," he looks down at the two sharks splayed open on a large lab table. "Looks like you've been making serious progress."

"Well, we won't have any results for several more hours, but I'm hoping the samples we've collected will tell us something useful. Why don't you help Brian over there with the dental work. I need as much material as possible for a viable DNA analysis; the samples need to be clean."

"Right, I'm on it," Falcon responds as he joins Brian. The young graduate student has been using a magnifying lamp to closely examine the rows of teeth that line the sharks' jaws. Then, using surgical tweezers, he has been carefully extracting the small bits of dried blood and tissue that are lodged in between.

As Falcon looks on, Brian brings him up to speed. "I've been finding quite a bit of tissue along the inside rows of teeth, Dr. Falcon. It appears to be the same type embedded in both the upper and lower mandibles. It looks to me like whatever this specimen fed on last was pretty large."

"Interesting observation, Brian, well done," agrees Falcon. He adjusts the large lens, then switches the light up to its highest setting. As he leans in close, the dead shark's jaws are just millimeters from his face. "I never cease to be fascinated by the magnificent engineering of this animal," Falcon's voice softens almost to a whisper. "Like the way these rows of teeth perpetually grow throughout the shark's lifespan; as soon as any are lost, brand new ones replace them like a weapons assembly line. This individual is only an average specimen really, nothing spectacular, yet still remarkable."

"I agree, Dr. Falcon, they're incredible creatures." Brian watches carefully as Falcon examines the specimen. "Hey, wait, did you see that?"

Falcon stops. "Brian, what did you see?"

"I don't know. It was a flash, as you moved the light; I saw a glimmer or something,"

"Really? That is interesting. You stay in that position, Brian; I'll move the light again." Falcon adjusts the light once more, the same way he had a few seconds before.

"Yes, I just saw it again, it's right there. Do you see it?"

Falcon raises up to the student's angle of view, then moves the light again. "Yes, I do. Just a second, let me grab the tweezers."

Digging down in between the second and third rows of blood-stained teeth, Falcon locates the source of the mysterious flash, then using the tweezers carefully plucks it out.

"Oh my god," Falcon gasps as he raises the tweezers up in front of his face while Brian looks on.

"It's a diamond stud earring."

* * *

The next day Marsh and Falcon are in the lab with Alex Moss, Malcolm Rafferty, and two senior officers from the Philippine Coast Guard. Dr. Peter Marsh speaks for the team: "We all worked through the night on this. What we found is disturbing, but we hope this information will help to forward your investigation of this tragedy," Marsh hands a file folder of data to the ranking officer. "The specimens were highly decomposed," Marsh continues, "however, we were still able to extract enough tissue to complete our analysis."

This particular ranking officer was sent by his superiors due to his own background in marine biology. The officer has the file open, he listens to Marsh as he scans the file's contents. "The DNA you extracted from the tissue embedded in the teeth of the sharks was human, yet the contents of the stomach and digestive tract contained no human remains?"

"That is correct, sir. Dr. Falcon and I each performed complete necropsies on all four specimens. We ran two separate sets of samples just to be sure, and both sample sets yielded identical results.

"The tissue collected from the teeth of the sharks clearly showed human DNA, leading us to conclude they indeed attacked the people on that cruise ship. We also found the DNA of multiple individuals in each sample, indicating the sharks each attacked multiple victims. What is puzzling is why we found no human remains in the stomachs of any of them. This fact is inconsistent with what we would consider to be normal shark behavior, and for this inconsistency we currently don't have an answer. As you are no doubt aware, sir, a predator kills in order to feed. Despite the sensationalism surrounding sharks, the idea that they are mindless killers is a myth; on that fact I would stake my reputation as an expert in this field of study."

The officer then looks at Falcon. "And does your colleague Dr. Falcon agree with this analysis?"

"Absolutely, sir. Dr. Marsh is one of the world's most highly respected ichthyologists. His expertise is well recognized."

"Well then," the officer steps forward, he reaches out to shake hands with each of the two scientists. "Dr. Marsh, Dr. Falcon, on behalf of my superiors and the government of the Philippines, we would like to thank you for your contribution to this investigation."

Moss and Rafferty escort the two officers from the lab, leading them back out on deck, where three Coast Guard seamen have been waiting for them with a RIB to take them back to their ship. As the officers approach the gangway leading down to the RIB, however, Moss can see the ranking officer has more he wants to tell him. "Is there anything else we can do for you, sir?"

"You are very perceptive, Mr. Moss; I didn't want to share this information publicly in front of your team in the lab. In light of this most recent attack, we are now on full alert. We've been in contact with the U.S. Navy base, and our own military has been put on alert. We will soon issue an advisory to all commercial shipping traffic; we've cordoned off a two-hundred-square mile restricted zone around the cruise ship, and we will issue a warning to stay clear of this area until further notice. This includes your ship, Mr. Moss. We appreciate all that you've done here, but my advice would be to leave this area immediately."

As the officers board the RIB and depart for the Coast Guard cutter waiting nearby, Moss turns to Rafferty. "I was hoping it wouldn't come to this, Razz, but after we get underway, go tap Murray and Seth, open up the weapons compartment. We've got work to do."

Chapter 15

The weapons compartment on board *Fearless* was designed and constructed under the direction of Alex Moss himself. The heavy welding was completed by the crew during a three-week stay in a lonely dry dock in Colon, Panama. All with the full backing of the Foundation's board of directors. The ship was brand new at the time, just three months out from her launch in Bremerhaven, Germany, on the North Sea.

None of her paramilitary features were added at the shipyard, however, under the specific direction of Moss himself, in order that her secrets remained off of any blueprints. The ship's weapons compartment is roughly the size of a small shipping container, its location and shape mimicking the dimensions of one of the ship's four main fuel tanks. Access is gained through a well-hidden, electronically secured hatch in the floor of the engine room.

The weapons themselves have been acquired more slowly, however, accumulated over the past four years that *Fearless* has been fully operational as a commercially licensed, research and expeditionary vessel. She has now circumnavigated the planet, during which time Moss, through a network of well-connected military buddies, has taken advantage of the ship's official itinerary.

During stops in Bahrain, Turkey, Israel, Jordan, and South Africa, allowing the former SEAL choice opportunities to stockpile an extensive collection of small arms and ammunition.

Other than during strictly controlled maintenance, however, the compartment is kept securely locked. Only Moss and Rafferty know the access code. During the past four years, there has only been one other incident that required the compartment be opened in order to defend the ship from attack. Other than that, the compartment's contents haven't been used for anything other than training exercises. Moss had always hoped that would be the way things would remain.

"So what's our plan?" Rafferty asks as he and Moss head back up to the bridge after seeing the Coast Guard on their way.

"First priority is to offload the science personnel. I don't want any of the civilian staff put in harm's way if we can help it. There's a commercial marina one hundred and twenty miles south of here; it's within an hour taxi ride of an airport."

"Good idea," Rafferty says as he glances at his watch, then after some quick mental calculations, continues: "If we leave now we should make it there by tomorrow morning pretty easily."

"It also puts us well outside the restricted zone the Coast Guard has established. I just hope it's far enough, but if it isn't, I want to be ready. You hear me, Razz?"

"Yeah, I hear you."

* * *

Down in the lab, Alistair and Brian are cleaning up after the science team's late night shark necropsy marathon. "What did Dr. Marsh say to do with these carcasses?" Alistair asks.

"He said to freeze them," answers Brian as he mops the floor with bleach. "Dr. Marsh feels we will need to reexamine them at some point. These could be the only physical specimens we are able to get our hands on; they're much too important. We have to preserve them."

Alistair looks down at the body bag containing the remains of the four dead sharks. It's been resealed, after the bag was thoroughly cleaned, then catalogued and labeled by Peter Marsh himself. "Wow, I hope the kitchen doesn't try to make soup or something…" At that moment a smelly wet sponge flies across the room, hitting Alistair squarely in the side of his head. "Shit!" Alistair shouts. "I just took a shower! Brian, you are so dead, man; you are seriously dead."

"Yeah, sure, you want a piece of this?" Brian taunts as he kicks the mop handle to the floor, then signals Alistair to make his move.

"Hey guys, ok, enough already…" Slightly irritated, Marsh enters the lab, pulling an empty hand truck behind him.

"Sorry Dr. Marsh," the two students speak in unison as if they were still in the third grade.

Marsh wheels the hand truck over next to the table the body bag is now resting on. "Give me a hand here, guys. The kitchen has very kindly cleared out a section of their walk-in freezer; I don't want to keep them waiting, ok?"

Marsh and the two students load the bag onto the hand truck, then haul it upstairs to the galley where they pack it carefully in the far corner of the walk-in. Just as they're leaving the galley, the trio pick up the unmistakable rumbling, clanking sound of the ship's anchors being raised.

"Mr. Moss is moving the ship," says Marsh. "You two get back down to the lab, finish cleaning up. I'm going to find out where we're off to."

Marsh is on his way to the bridge when he meets up with Falcon, who also received the signal that *Fearless* would soon be on the move. Falcon picks up his pace in order to match that of Marsh.

"So what do you think is their plan?" asks Falcon. "Have you heard anything from Mr. Moss?"

"No, I haven't," answers Marsh, "and I couldn't begin to guess, but I'm disappointed, really. I was hoping to stay close by." Marsh stops walking. "Tom, you and I both know we don't have all of the necessary facts required to publish. We have to observe this phenomenon directly, first hand. It's the only way to collect the proper data and get the answers we need."

Falcon looks directly at his friend. "I agree, Peter, but there's also the safety of the ship to consider. To be honest, I'm not at all excited about the prospect of coming face to face with the mob that killed those cruise ship passengers. Are you?"

"When you put it like that, Tom, I'd have to agree; I don't either, and I see your point, old friend, and honestly it's the reason I invited you out here in the first place. I've always appreciated your sense of clarity. Sometimes I get so lost in the work..." Marsh pauses; he looks at Falcon, then puts his hand on the other man's shoulder. "I just want to say thank you, I'm really glad you're here."

On the bridge, Moss is directing operations as the ship's mammoth twin anchors lock into their storage positions, deep niches that flank either side of the bow. Rafferty is out on deck, supervising the crew as they complete their assigned checklists.

The men work together to secure hatches and stow equipment in preparation for departure. Marsh enters the bridge followed by Falcon, but Moss waves them off. "Not now, gentlemen; we're underway. I'll get back to you in a few minutes." His tone of voice is even, measured, almost mechanical, his mind totally focused on the operation. He is at the center of a complex constellation of actions that all must be completed in perfect synchronization.

Marsh and Falcon stand out of the way, observing quietly as Moss takes his position beside his helmsman, quietly directing his actions as Moss alternates between glances at the radar display, the wind and depth readings, and the ship's large touchscreen navigational plotter. All while simultaneously exchanging brief, precise radio communications with the observer positioned at the bow, the second man he has stationed at the stern, and Rafferty midship. Moss smoothly conducts an orchestra of movement as the three-hundred-and-eighteen-foot-long vessel performs her delicate dance under his direction.

The low hum of her engines is hardly perceptible as *Fearless* moves slowly forward. Moss then gently increases speed as she approaches the pass that marks the entrance to the bay in which they had been anchored. They follow the channel markers out into the open sea, where, once the ship is clear of the bay, Moss turns to Falcon and Marsh. "Gentlemen, I apologize that I wasn't able to inform you of our departure in advance. Unfortunately, we are operating under an evacuation protocol as a result of this most recent attack. The Coast Guard has issued a directive to all ships in this region to leave this area immediately.

"If you take a look here, I can show you our planned route," Moss directs as he steps over to the chart table; Marsh and Falcon follow. Moss then points to an area he's marked on the chart. "This area outlined on the chart is now under restricted access as designated by the local authorities. I have no choice but to respect the order. I have our new course plotted." Moss points to the area of the chart that shows the bay they just departed from. "We were here. As you can see, we are currently inside the restricted zone. So we plan to sail one hundred twenty-four miles south, to this bay. This puts us over fifty miles clear of the Coast Guard's directive. We will arrive by 0700 tomorrow, where the Foundation's travel office has accommodation, transfers and flights waiting for you and…"

"Wait, hold on!" blurts a startled Marsh. "You're pitching us off?" Falcon says nothing; he's equally stunned by this surprise development but also secretly relieved.

Moss sighs. "Look, Dr. Marsh, I'm sorry, but the safety of this ship and her crew are my responsibility. This was my call."

"But what about my work? The grant? Has it been rescinded?"

"No, absolutely not. The board has asked me to inform you the grant is still fully funded. After we have this situation resolved, they would like you to return. For now, however, it's too dangerous to keep you and your team on board. I know this is difficult. It was a hard decision to make, but I feel it's the right thing to do. I hope you can understand my position."

Marsh is devastated by the decision, but he respects Alex Moss too much to argue about it. "I do understand your position, Mr. Moss. I'll inform my team. Now, if you'll excuse us, we have packing to do."

Moss calls out to the two men as they begin to leave: "Dr. Marsh, I appreciate your cooperation, and I look forward to having you back on board once we have this situation cleared up." As he speaks, Moss extends his hand toward Marsh.

Marsh turns to look Moss in the eye, then, reaching out, he grips Moss' hand firmly. "Thank you, I appreciate that very much."

Chapter 16

The sparkling silver light of a full moon dances across a flat calm sea as *Fearless* steadily motors on. It's three in the morning. Peter Marsh stands at the railing. He breathes in the salt-laced night air as he looks out at the beautiful scene with sadness. He has spent six months aboard this incredible vessel, yet not once has he taken the time to really enjoy the fact that he is at sea. He had been too busy, too focused on the work. Now he is leaving. He takes a sip from the beer he pilfered from the galley fridge and watches as bright green sparks of phosphorescent plankton light up in the ship's frothy wake. The ethereal glow rushes by like a river past the hull of the ship; he has regrets, and he wishes he didn't.

* * *

Alone in his cabin, Thomas Falcon kneels in front of a small shrine he has constructed to honor his grandmother and the ancestors of his family that passed before her. He feels awkward; this is all very foreign and strange. He is embarrassed, actually, but at the same time what he is doing feels necessary. Like something he has to do, even though he wishes he didn't.

The photo of the little boy smiling as he sits on the lap of his grandmother is in front of him. She holds him close, her arms wrapped tightly around him; the image has always given Falcon comfort. He stares at it for a while; he doesn't know how long, really. His cabin is lit only by two small candles. He looks at them as well; he looks again at the photograph. Then he becomes lost.

He's not sure where he is. Perhaps the candles have gone out, or he's fallen asleep. He doesn't know, but suddenly he is awake. Falcon soon realizes he is no longer in his cabin; he's in the sea, on his solo night dive to the kill-zone one hundred feet deep. Falcon looks up at the shimmering surface of the ocean lit by soft moonlight far above him. He watches as the stream of bubbles rising from his regulator reflect in the moon's glow. He can see the clear outline of *Fearless*, with her anchor chains trailing out in front of her.

Falcon looks around. He sees the white sand reflecting the moonlight, the coral heads standing like dark sentinels, and hundreds upon hundreds of dead sharks. No fear rises inside of him this time, he feels no panic, no anger either; he feels only sadness. Falcon swims out over the rotting corpses of the dead sharks. Then, right in front of him, resting on her side, just as he'd first found her, lies the massive body of the female tiger shark.

Falcon stops; he knows this is where he is supposed to be. So he waits. Suddenly, from behind a coral head, a sea snake appears. It's beautiful, incredibly colored; it seems to glow somehow. The snake's appearance is astonishing. Falcon recognizes it from the stories his grandmother used to tell: This is the rainbow serpent, the messenger between the spirit world and the physical world. Falcon becomes mesmerized as he watches the snake swim around him. It dances and darts between Falcon and the tiger shark as it touches and tastes with its rapidly flipping tongue; then it approaches him.

Instinctively Falcon reaches out his hand, and a surge of energy passes through him as the snake tastes his skin with its tongue. Instantly Falcon is back in Jamaica. He is standing in the back yard of his grandmother's house. It's a sunny tropical day, and he is surrounded by the bright colors of her garden. He can smell the fragrance of gardenia blossoms carried by the sea breeze. He can hear the coconut palms rustling above him. He looks down to see he is wearing his Sunday suit. Then he looks up to see his grandmother coming out through the back door onto her porch; she is also dressed for Sunday.

"Thomas," she calls to him softly, "are you ready for church?"

"Yes Gramma," he answers. Then Falcon's grandmother walks out across the yard toward him. She comes to him, then takes his hands in hers, and looks deeply into his eyes.

"Thomas, it wasn't your fault this happened. I didn't teach you, and I should have, and I'm sorry for that, but now is the time to make things right."

"What should I do? There's so much I want to ask you; there's so much you need to tell me."

"Shush now, just listen; we don't have time for all that. Thomas, you must appease the spirit you have offended; it's the only way, Thomas. You must take back the talisman; you must get it back. It's the only way. Do you understand me?"

"Yes Gramma, I understand."

At that moment Falcon finds himself back in his cabin. He's still sitting on the floor with the candles still burning in front of him. He stands up, blows out the candles, and takes apart the shrine. Then he goes to find Peter Marsh.

Chapter 17

At 0400 every morning, the galley awakens as the kitchen staff aboard *Fearless* start their day. First order of business is to get the coffee going as the chief likes his hot and fresh as soon as he wakes up. Second order of business are the buttermilk biscuits. A staple on board, each day they're mixed from scratch and baked fresh. The next most important breakfast staple being fried bacon, and lots of it, as the crew enjoy a thick stack inside chef's delectably fluffy biscuits.

As the chef begins his standard routine of preparing enough biscuits to satisfy a ship load of military-grade appetites, he passes by the large stainless steel tray that is supposed to have four and a half kilos of defrosted raw bacon sitting on it, but this tray is empty. "Shit…" He calls to his line cook, who is busy loading flour into an industrial-sized mixer. "Charlie, who was on duty last night? They forgot to take the bacon out of the freezer. Can you go get it?"

"Yeah, yeah, I got it, don't get your panties in a wad…" Charlie puts down the large flour sack, then heads for the ship's walk-in freezer. He pulls hard on the handle, opens the thick heavy door, then pushes aside a row of clear plastic strips hanging across the doorway as a blast of frigid air assaults his senses. Charlie walks inside, irritated that the first thing he's gotta do this morning is go into the goddamn freezer. The wrapped and pre-measured stacks of bacon are on a shelf just inside the door. He reaches up and pulls one of the ten-pound blocks from the shelf when he hears something.

Charlie pauses, the chunk of frozen bacon numbing his fingers as he listens... there... he hears it again. He shoves the bacon back onto the shelf, then looks to find what's making the noise. It seems to be getting louder; a rustling sound coming from the far corner of the walk-in. Reaching back, Charlie flips on the overhead light. He sees the body bag the science team left behind, and it appears to be moving. There's something inside. "What the hell?" Charlie is disgusted. "I never wanted this shit near my food to begin with," he grumbles. "Goddamn hippie science freaks..." He walks over to the thrashing bag. "What the hell is this shit..."

Charlie leans over and attempts to unzip the bag, but it's frozen shut, so he gets down on his knees for a better grip. Pulling hard, he manages to open the bag about a third of the way down. The body bag is still moving as Charlie pulls back the sides to reveal the frosted remains of the four dead sharks. "What the fuck?" He looks down at the milky white dead eye of the shark lying on top. Its jaws are partially open, its teeth crusted over with frost, when suddenly its body shifts. "Jesus Martha!" Charlie shouts, he falls backwards, his heels slipping on the frozen rubber floor mat as he scrambles to get away. Then, rolling onto his hands and knees, he attempts to get to his feet when something suddenly hits him hard from behind.

Searing pain shoots up through Charlie's body as he turns to see a near-frozen shark biting into his lower leg. Charlie lets out a scream just as the chef is walking into the freezer to find out what all the commotion is about. "My god!" the chef shouts. He spins around and runs out, returning instantly with a large cleaver. "Charlie!" the chef yells, "try not to move. Let me get a clean shot!" The chef levels the cleaver dead center into the head of the shark, burying the blade deep into the shark's decomposed flesh where it becomes instantly stuck. As the chef struggles to pull the cleaver out again, the shark fights back. Its head thrashes back and forth with the cleaver sticking out of it, as the chef desperately tries to maintain his grip on the cleaver's handle. Neither of the two men notice that the other three sharks have now freed themselves from the body bag. "Hold on Charlie, I've gotta get help!" the chef shouts, as he runs from the freezer to the ship's comm mounted on a wall nearby.

On the bridge, Rafferty has a chart spread out on the large mahogany table that is the centerpiece of the room. He is in the process of laying out the mooring options to Moss once Fearless arrives. Although the ship is fully equipped with the latest in touchscreen digital chart plotters, Moss has always been a big picture kind of guy, preferring the old school paper navigational charts. Rafferty points to the harbor they had planned to moor in. "They don't have room for us in the marina on this short notice. Unsurprisingly, there's a lot of boat traffic heading south at the moment, but this next bay just a half mile away looks like a good anchorage..."

"Chief!" a crewman shouts as he runs through the door.

Moss looks up. "Randy, What's happening?"

"We just got a call into the infirmary; it came from the galley. They're being attacked..."

Moss looks quizzically at the crewmen. "Attacked?"

"Yeah, it seems crazy, but chef says those sharks in the freezer are attacking them."

Moss looks at Rafferty. "I'll go check this out. You find Dr. Marsh and Dr. Falcon. Meet me down in the galley." Then Moss points at Randy. "You're with me," he barks. "Let's go."

Marsh is in his cabin, staring once more at his computer screen, evaluating what he's just written, knowing that the words only come easily when you don't care what anyone else thinks. He reaches for his steaming tea mug, and is taking a sip as someone knocks on his door.

"Peter, am I disturbing you?"

"Tom, no, of course not, come in."

Falcon takes a seat on the edge of the bunk as he rubs his hands nervously across his knees.

"What's going on? The last time I saw you like this was just before we sat for exams."

"Peter, I've got something very serious to tell you."

"What? What is it? Tom, please I've had enough bad news for one day."

"I'm just going to say it, Peter, there's no other way... Do you remember when Mr. Moss discovered someone on board had made an unauthorized dive?"

"I knew it was you!" Marsh chuckles. "You always had that stealth ability. Remember that time we snuck into..."

"Peter, not now, please..."

Marsh stops laughing. He sighs, then looks seriously at Falcon. "Ok then, have at it. What's going on?"

"These shark attacks, I know what they are..."

"Seriously? You have a theory? Please do share, old friend."

"No, not a theory…" Falcon pauses; he knows he's about to cross a line that can never be uncrossed. "I know what they are because I caused all this, or better to say, something I did started this whole nightmare going."

Marsh looks at Falcon with dumbfounded exasperation. "Tom, I can't even begin to imagine what you're talking about…"

At that moment there's another knock on the door followed by a hurried voice from outside: "Dr. Marsh, can I speak to you?"

Marsh rolls his chair quickly within reach of the door handle and pops it open.

"Mr. Rafferty, what can I do for you?"

"Sorry to disturb you, Dr. Marsh," Rafferty steps inside, where he sees Falcon is also there. "Dr. Falcon, good. The chief sent me down to fetch you guys. There's some sort of problem with those sharks you left in the freezer. We need you immediately."

Falcon looks at Marsh. "We'd better go right now. If it's what I think it is, we're in serious trouble."

Marsh and Falcon follow Rafferty as they head quickly up to the galley. They reach the main corridor in time to hear a man screaming. "Oh dear god," Falcon whispers as the three men run the rest of the way. Bounding through the crew mess, then pushing through the swinging door that leads to the kitchen, they find Moss and Randy fighting off three viciously attacking zombie sharks. Moss glances across the room and sees Rafferty.

"Razz! I could use a hand here!"

Without missing a step, Rafferty grabs an oversized cast aluminum meat mallet hanging from a utility rack then begins pounding the head of the shark that's now biting into Randy's knee. Moss continues to battle the remaining two sharks; he's armed with a pair of large chef's knives. Moss has one shark nearly out of commission, but the second is still fighting. Meanwhile Falcon spots a commercial-sized stick blender lying on a work surface. He picks up the hefty kitchen tool, then briefly examines it: "Cordless, stainless steel blades," he mutters as he flips it on, "and fully charged."

Without hesitation Falcon runs to where Moss is still stabbing at the shark. "Look out!" Falcon shouts as he shoves the spinning blades into the shark's gills. He pushes hard against the heavy mixer's long barrel, as it powers its way deep into the shark's rotted body. The blades are effective, but they also spray the kitchen with rotted slime and half-frozen rancid flesh as the spinning steel blades slice into the reanimated corpse. The motor whines as the blades grind through skeletal cartilage until the shark finally stops moving. Falcon stares down at the remains, his hands go limp as the machine leaves his grip and drops to the floor.

Falcon then looks up at a furiously enraged Moss still gripping the two knives. Rafferty says nothing; he immediately turns away to seek help for Randy, the injured crewman. Falcon then steps back from the carcass as Marsh breaks the silence.

"What's happening?" Marsh shouts in astonishment. "What's going on here?"

Moss, breathing heavily, and still tightly gripping the two large chef's knives, points one of them toward Falcon. "You better ask your friend here… What's that you called it, Dr. Falcon? *Reanimation?*"

Meanwhile, in the back of the kitchen, Rafferty is on the comm to the ship's medic. "No Seth, I'm not kidding, we've got serious injuries; you better get down here right away." Rafferty then grabs a stack of towels from a shelf and tends to the wounded crewman.

Marsh, completely exasperated, looks at Falcon. "Tom, what is he talking about? I don't understand any of this. How can these sharks be attacking anyone? They're dead! We performed necropsies! We froze them, for Christ's sake!"

Moss looks at Falcon as sweat drips down his forehead and the veins on his temples pulse; he's on the verge of losing control. "I've got two men dead inside that freezer, another man wounded, and I want answers now, Dr. Falcon. You have my full attention, sir. What should we be expecting here? What's coming for us?"

Falcon glances at Peter Marsh, then focuses on Moss. His words are measured and even as he speaks: "What attacked the fishing boat, the beach resort, and the cruise ship was a zombie horde. These sharks aren't really sharks anymore; they have no mind of their own, they have no fear, no sense of self-preservation, they're zombies, reanimated corpses being driven by the talisman carried by the tiger shark I told you about."

"And let me guess," Moss hisses, "they're heading this way? How many of them are there, Dr. Falcon? How many *zombies* did you unleash?"

Falcon sighs. "It's hard to say, exactly; the energy field generated by the talisman, it's extremely powerful. It appears the horde has been growing, which means the energy field must be expanding. This has to be what awakened the sharks in the freezer, and this means the horde must be close, possibly very close. There could be thousands by now. It's difficult to…"

Alex Moss has just been pushed beyond his breaking point. He drops the two knives to the floor as he lunges at Falcon. Thrusting a thickly muscled forearm, he seizes Falcon by the throat then shoves him up against a wall. "I've got men dead here!" Moss roars. "I've spent my life cleaning up disasters created by men like you who insist on setting fires they can't control!"

Moss catches himself. He freezes, then he releases Falcon, who falls to his knees gasping. Moss then turns to Rafferty, who is holding pressure on Randy's bleeding leg.

"How's he doing?"

Razz looks up at Moss. "It's not too bad. The medic's on his way."

"As soon as Seth arrives, meet me upstairs; I'm assembling the crew for a briefing. I need you there."

Rafferty gives a quick nod of acknowledgement. Moss then storms out of the kitchen, leaving Falcon collapsed on the floor struggling to breathe. Meanwhile Peter Marsh stands motionless in a stunned state of cognitive dissidence. As Falcon regains his wind, he reaches up and grips the edge of a sink, then slowly pulls himself back to his feet. Seeing Falcon struggling, Marsh rushes in and grabs Falcon's arm to steady him as he stands,

"Are you ok, old friend?"

Falcon then looks at Marsh. "I am afraid I am no longer anyone's friend…"

Chapter 18

On the bridge, Moss has his core crew assembled, minus Randy, and his lead pilot, who's still with the ship's chopper in Manila. The ten remaining men standing before him were hand-picked, recruited by Moss personally. All of them had served in various combat theaters around the world, and most have now been with *Fearless* since her launch four years ago.

They were chosen not only for their seamanship abilities, but also due to specialized skill sets they each possess, such as technical diving and undersea welding, research remotely operated underwater vehicle (ROV) and submarine operations, a second helicopter pilot, as well as small arms, explosives, hand to hand and close-quarter combat. Moss stands behind the chart table, his arms folded in front of him as the men gathered around look on, then Rafferty enters, giving a quick glance as Moss begins:

"Gentlemen, in light of recent developments we have a change in plans." Moss pauses, then places his hands on the edge of the table. "First off, as most of you are already aware, we just had an attack take place. It originated in the galley freezer resulting in one injury and two fatalities. The shark specimens flown in by the Coast Guard for examination by our science team were not ordinary sharks as we previously thought. "Apparently, being dead does not preclude these particular sharks from being able to fatally attack someone." Moss pauses once more; he lifts his hands to his hips, and quickly evaluates the reaction from his crew. "Yes, this indeed seems crazy, but as Mr. Rafferty will confirm, he and I were forced to defend ourselves against three of them just twenty minutes ago. Unfortunately, I can assure you they are extremely dangerous."

Moss then pauses for a moment. Leaning in toward the group, he places his hands back on the edge of the table and allows for what he's just said to sink in as he evaluates the effectiveness of his presentation. Quickly scanning the faces of the men, Moss is satisfied that his message is getting across, so he continues. "The safety of this ship and everyone on board has always been our first priority. Gentlemen, we are now under threat. We have received actionable intelligence that what attacked that cruise ship, is now coming after us.

"In light of what has just happened, we are skipping our planned stop. Instead, we will continue south and remain near the coast until we reach the U.S. Naval base at Subic, where we will seek shelter. Until then this ship is on full security alert. Mr. Rafferty has previously prepared the weapons compartment. He has informed me all weapons are service ready. Everyone knows their assigned duties; we'll stick to the drill for now, but be ready to improvise. As I know more, so will you. Now let's get to work, gentlemen."

* * *

Dawn breaks and the placid sea is a liquid mirror. The early light paints a row of thick clouds on the horizon crimson as the sun rises. Malcolm Rafferty is watching from the bridge, his mind flooded with thoughts. Mostly, he's been thinking about his ex-wife Robyn and his son Mark, and how he wishes his family life could have turned out differently. He knows the real reason why of course, the reason why Robyn just couldn't take it. It was because of all the times in his life, too many actually, all the moments like this that he'd experienced. All of the missions that she was forced to live through from a distance, never knowing where he was going, or if he would come back. Meanwhile, he would be somewhere, usually uncomfortable, watching the sunrise, thinking about her, and waiting for a battle to begin.

Whether it was a damp, insect-infested jungle in Colombia, or Indonesia, a dry scrub forest in Sudan, perched on the side of an unnamed frozen mountain in Afghanistan, or holed up on a rooftop in some bleak, hopeless village in Iraq; where he happened to be never mattered. Completing the mission mattered. Keeping himself and his team alive mattered the most. *It's true*, he thinks to himself, *it pays to be a winner... but what does being a winner really mean?*

Rafferty isn't fooling himself; he knows his youth is behind him. All of the guys on board are long retired from special operations. They are no longer part of the teams and no longer the brash young men they once were. The certainty Rafferty had always felt before previous operations is not present, and it bothers him.

Lost in thought, Malcolm Rafferty misses the first transmission over the common emergency radio channel. The second one, however, catches his attention; a pan-pan sent out from a freighter asking for assistance due to a serious medical emergency. Rafferty reaches over and rolls up the volume a few clicks on the radio. He then waits and listens for the freighter to repeat the message. A few moments go by before the pan-pan comes through again. It's the same freighter; her crew are repeating the previous transmission, but this time with more detail; they have three crew seriously injured by sharks. Rafferty snaps to attention. He grabs a pen and notepad and quickly scribbles down the ship's position and checks it against the current position of *Fearless* on the plotter; the freighter is only nine nautical miles behind them.

* * *

Falcon is resting on his bunk when he hears a knock on his door. "Tom, it's me..." Opening the door, he sees Marsh.

"Peter, I'm afraid I really don't have much to say..."

Marsh enters. "Tom, look... I just wanted to apologize. I wasn't much help back there..."

Falcon is surprised. "Peter, what on earth are you talking about? I'm the one who should be apologizing here. I'm the one who caused all of this in the first place. Two men on this ship are dead because of me, and countless others... Peter, there's no forgiving something like this—not ever."

Marsh sighs, then slowly leans back against the door. "Tom, I really refuse to believe you somehow caused all of this. It's an utterly ludicrous claim as far as I'm concerned, and I can't imagine how you've come to this conclusion but..." Marsh puts his hands together, he raises them up to his chin momentarily as he quickly gathers his thoughts. "But... let's just say you're right. I saw those sharks attacking the men in the galley, Tom. *I saw them*. And as much as I want to disbelieve what I've just personally witnessed, I can't. So please tell me how this has happened, Tom, explain it to me because I need to know what's going on here. What I'm really hoping is that, knowing you, whenever we were up against what seemed like an untenable problem, you could always find a solution. So tell me, Tom, do we have any sort of chance against this 'horde' as you call it? Is there a solution, Tom?"

Falcon looks at Marsh with resolve. "Yes, there is a solution, but I have to do it alone, and it won't be easy…"

* * *

Down in the weapons compartment, Moss supervises as three crewmen prepare to distribute arms, ammunition, tactical uniforms, and body armor from the ship's hidden cache. Even after the fight in the kitchen, however, Moss is still trying to reconcile the fact that they're evaluating weapons and strategy to determine which will be the most effective against an approaching horde of zombie sharks.

Moss takes a German-made Heckler and Koch MP5 submachine gun down from a storage rack containing twenty of them. The ubiquitous companion of special forces around the world, it's a weapon Moss is intimately familiar with. "I've never had to plan a counter insurgency against a bunch of reanimated dead fish," Moss quips sarcastically as he inspects the gun's folding stock and sight adjustments. "But based on what happened down in the galley, inflict enough physical damage, and it seems to disrupt the energy field that drives them, rendering the individual animal inoperable, so I'm open to suggestions, gentlemen. Any ideas?"

"Hey, Chief," asks Steve, a fellow SEAL, who's known Moss for eight years, he holds up a Belgian-made FN Herstal P90, a stubby-looking personal defense weapon designed specifically for close quarter combat. Used extensively by NATO troops, its top-mounted clip holds fifty rounds, but the P90 is capable of firing nine hundred rounds a minute. "These ugly beasties can really do some damage, and we have enough to issue them to everyone on board."

"I agree, but I don't want any civilians carrying guns, is that clear? We have enough to worry about."

Then Murray, an Australian SAS alumni, pulls a crate packed with military-grade Tasers and stun batons from a shelf. "If it's an energy field controlling them, then maybe these could be effective in disrupting it." Murray shoves the box back, then reaches up for another crate. "And... we've also got these," he pulls out a second crate, this one containing XREP long range shells. The XREP is a self-contained electrical stun cartridge with a wireless range of thirty meters. Murray pulls one of the shells from its box. "These pesky nippers can be fired from those SLPs over there," he gestures toward another impressively outfitted storage rack on the opposite side of the room, this one containing, among other lethal wares, several FN Herstal-made tactical twelve-gauge shotguns. "This stuff's all pretty flash... what do you think, Chief?"

"Worth a try. Issue those to..." As Moss speaks, Rafferty's voice cuts in; it's coming from the handheld radio clipped to Moss' belt. Moss grabs the radio and responds:

"What's happening Razz?"

"We're receiving emergency transmissions from other ships in the area, better get up here."

Moss turns to the other men. "Get these weapons distributed. I want everyone suited up and at their stations." Moss then slings two of the MP5s over his shoulder as Steve hands him a bag containing several clips and a pair of P90s, then he gestures toward the Tasers.

"How about these?"

Moss gives the Tasers a quick glance, then he reaches past Steve, and instead grabs a holster containing a pair of large, long-handled, Kukri blades. Commonly referred to as Gurkha blades, this set was hand forged from Damascus steel by a skilled traditional sword smith in Afghanistan under Moss's personal direction. The impressively sized, ax-shaped Kukris eventually became his trademark during his last tour of duty there. Moss hangs the holster containing the deadly edged weapons over his shoulder. "I'll be on the bridge if you need me, gentlemen."

As Moss leaves, the three crewmen look at each other, each grinning slyly as Murray announces, "Zombies beware, the Ax is back."

Chapter 19

Moss enters the bridge. He calmly places the weapons and gear he's carrying under the chart table as the ship's VHF screams with maritime emergency DSC alarms. Known as Digital Selective Calling, it's a type of emergency automated radio required on all commercial vessels. Moss attempts to discern the scramble of overlapping human voices and electronic signals. Rafferty looks up from the nav-station. "There's too many to deal with, Ax. So far I've plotted the position of seven separate vessels sending out Mayday calls. Based on the volume of radio traffic, there's probably more. The Coast Guard is overwhelmed; they just keep sending out general evacuation orders. All they can do now is try to warn ships to stay out of the area."

Moss checks the chart plotter that's now crowded with small triangular shapes representing various ships' AIS—automated identification signals—while the coordinates of known ships in distress plotted by Rafferty show up as small dots. "Looks like all of the ships in distress are still north of our position. How far are we from the naval base?"

"Still over fifty miles," answers Rafferty.

Moss looks up from the plotter. "We have daylight and flat seas. Tell the guys on deck to keep a close watch and report anything they see. We're making good speed. We stick to the plan; as soon as we get within range I'll contact the base."

On deck eight crewmen, now fully armed, patrol the ship's perimeter. The two men assigned to the ship's forward section scan the horizon as a velvet, carpet-like sea glides smoothly under the prow of *Fearless*. The late morning sun now radiating an intensity that foretells the heat of the coming day as the crew vigilantly keep watch. Then the two men at the bow see something, a dark line slowly becoming visible across the horizon; it looks like a large wave. One of the men quickly radios the bridge: "Chief, forward deck, we've spotted something."

"On my way," Moss snaps back, then quickly adds, "Everyone else, hold your positions."

On the bow, Moss stands with the two crewmen as he carefully evaluates the mysterious wave, which appears to be several hundred meters ahead of them. It forms a long undulating line stretching over a mile across.

"What do you think it is, Chief?" one of the men asks. "Do you think it's them?"

Moss squints as he peers through the binoculars. "We appear to be gaining on it, and it's traveling in our same direction..." He pauses as he adjusts the focus. "It's a bunch of dolphins." He hands the binoculars back to the crewman. "Hundreds of them, looks like they're on the run." He then radios the bridge, "It's just a large group of dolphins."

* * *

Down below, Marsh listens patiently as Falcon tells him of his encounter with the shaman on the beach, his vision quest, and how the talisman is at the center of it all...

"I have to be honest, Tom; if I hadn't seen the things I've seen over this past week, I would be politely dismissing your story as the ranting of a man whose mind is clearly broken. But the facts as they stand are clear. I did see the aftermath of two of these attacks, and I personally witnessed the incident in the galley. I have no reason to doubt what the local authorities have reported. I no longer doubt the video evidence we recovered. The necropsies make a bit more sense from a scientific viewpoint, and I certainly do not doubt the mental soundness of Mr. Moss.

"So tell me, old friend, how on earth do we get this talisman back? Have you seen the crew around here? They're armed to the teeth, Tom; these are soldiers preparing for war—this is some serious shit going on, mate. I had no idea they had such weaponry on board; it's frightening. So how on earth can we possibly get past all of these blokes, and... *AND*, also somehow find the one shark amongst a horde of thousands that happens to be carrying a tiny statue in her mouth? The odds are not in our favor, Tom. As a matter of fact, I venture to say the odds of success are as crazy as the circumstances that brought us here in the first place."

"So does this mean you're on board with my plan then, Peter?"

Marsh smiles meekly. "Well yes, then I guess it does."

Falcon stands. "I saw the latest announcement on the ship's intranet network; the kitchen is still closed, but the staff have made something called MREs available. We'd better get some food while we still can."

The two scientists head for the crew mess, but as they pass by a window, something outside catches Marsh's attention: "Hang on what's this?" Both men walk out on deck to see an extraordinarily massive group of dolphins, which are steadily being overtaken by *Fearless*. Hundreds of them now surround the ship on all sides; they leap through her wake and ride her bow wave. Falcon walks to the railing, joining Marsh, who is mesmerized by the spectacle.

"Look at that, it's a super pod. It's positively magnificent, isn't it, Tom? There must be a thousand of them. Look! They're all around us; it's incredible!" For a moment Peter Marsh forgets the horror they are facing, as he becomes lost in the magnificence of the sea life surrounding him. Then, unexpectedly, the entire gigantic pod changes direction; moving as if it were a single organism, the pod turns sharply away from shore as the dolphins swim for the open sea.

"Wow, that was quick!" Marsh exclaims.

Falcon stands quietly by as the fast-moving dolphins disappear into the distance. "They're on the run," Falcon says softly. "They know what's coming, and they know it's close."

Chapter 20

Down in the crew mess, several stacks of military MREs, or "meals ready to eat," sit on one of the dining tables along with a large, hotel-style coffee dispenser. A plastic bin full of small snacks—pretzels, chips, and candy—sits next to several rows of various canned sodas and bottled waters that have been arranged neatly along with a tray containing sugar packets, powdered creamer, plastic utensils, and a stack of paper cups. Aside from Marsh and Falcon, the room is empty. The remainder of the kitchen staff have been preoccupied with the sizable task of cleaning and sanitizing the disaster left behind by the deadly frozen shark incident. Bright yellow and black-striped caution tape is stretched across the kitchen's swinging front door. Marsh picks up one of the brick-sized sealed plastic food packs.

"This one says *Chili Con Carne*. What have you got, Tom?"

"Looks like I will be having the delicious *Salisbury Steak*. I don't imagine there's much of a difference really though, do you?"

"Probably not," Marsh answers as he tears open the heavy plastic outer bag, then watches with curiosity as a variety of smaller packets spill out onto his tray. "Well this is interesting," Marsh observes as he thumbs through the clearly labeled packages. "These certainly provide everything the soldier in the field might need. There's even a small dental kit and some chewing gum."

"Indeed," Falcon answers, "a far cry from the old days when all you got was a bit of tinned meat and some biscuits," as he dips a plastic fork into the room-temperature, processed food pack. "Mmmm... just like what dear old mum would make."

Just then Alistair and Brian enter the crew mess. Marsh looks up from his Chili Con Carne. "Hey guys, we were looking for you two; you almost missed breakfast."

"Oh no thanks, Dr. Marsh," Alistair answers. "We already tried a couple of those about an hour ago."

"We were looking for you, actually," adds Brian. "Have you seen all of the guns the crew have? These dudes are hardcore serious."

"It's a bit disturbing, I know, but just stay out of their way, ok guys? Mr. Moss informed me earlier that he would be giving a safety briefing shortly for the civilian staff and science personnel. He said he would be issuing us some defensive weapons just in case."

"Wow, cool! So do you think we'll get body armor too?" Alistair asks sarcastically.

"Oh yes," agrees Brian. "And I'd like one of those massive machine guns they're toting about, carried at a rakish angle, of course." As he speaks he strikes a dramatic pose, then pretends to brandish his imaginary weapon.

"No guns, gentlemen, at least not for us. Sorry, but Mr. Moss' orders, I'm afraid."

"And a good thing too, by the looks of it," adds Falcon, as he dumps the remains of his breakfast tray in the trash bin.

At that moment one of the crew walks in. It's Murray, formerly of the Australian SAS, and he's carrying a large duffle bag. "Right, and after just overhearing you two pups, I would have to agree with Dr. Falcon as well." Murray swings the heavy black nylon bag up onto one of the empty tables. "Ok, gather round, gentlemen, it's time for your safety briefing."

Marsh looks at Falcon, then at Murray. "But I thought…"

Murray quickly cuts in, "Yes, well, the Chief's pretty busy right now. He has his hands full upstairs trying to keep anyone else on board from getting killed. So let's get on with it; I haven't got all day."

The four men gather around the table as Murray rummages through the bag. "So for the two fish docs I've got…"

Marsh wades in: "Um… did you just call us *fish docs*?"

Murray glances up from the bag. "Oh, sorry, my bad… Um, well then, first off, the Chief wants all civilian personnel to remain in their cabins until we reach the American Navy base. This should take about four more hours. I see you chaps have had some grub, so that's taken care of. I strongly recommend you all carefully review the emergency procedures placard posted on the door of your cabins. You all remember the evacuation drill we had just after Dr. Falcon's arrival, right?"

The group nods in agreement as Murray looks at each one of them. "Well that's just super then, looks like you guys will do just fine. So let's move on then, shall we?" Murray begins pulling items from his bag. "Of course the Chief has everything well under control, and there's nothing to worry about. In the odd event things do go a bit pear-shaped, I have some very effective defensive tools for you guys. For, uh… Dr. Marsh and Dr. Falcon, I have these two Tasers," Murray hands each man a Taser and an instruction booklet. "I suggest you read the instructions carefully, gentlemen, and watch yourselves, these aren't toys; they're professional grade and fully charged." Marsh and Falcon both begin curiously examining the weapons they now hold in their hands.

"So what about us?" Alistair asks,

"Ah yes, well I've got some very special items for you two." Murray pulls out a pair of stun batons from his bag. "These stun batons are the business, so here you go, one for each of you, and there's a booklet of instructions that goes with these as well. Make sure you read it carefully. I'm sure you'll enjoy carrying these beauties at a rakish angle, right? Try not to practice on each other," Murray grins as he elbows Alistair.

Brian looks at his stun baton, then he attempts to peek further into the duffle bag. "Well, is that all then? Is this all we get?"

"Oh right, I almost forgot," Murray reaches for the bag, "and for all four of you, here's an emergency headlamp, and... a safety whistle." Murray passes out a light and whistle to each of the men. "So briefing's complete. Any questions? Great! Please proceed to your cabins immediately, and as soon as we have the all clear from the bridge, you'll be the first to know. So off you go now, have a nice day!" Murray zips the bag closed, swings it back up onto his shoulder and walks out, leaving the four men feeling oddly confused and somewhat offended.

"Well that was certainly interesting," Falcon says as he holds up the Taser.

"Wanna trade, Dr. Marsh?" asks Alistair as he swings the baton by its strap.

"Guys, please, enough jokes, ok?" Marsh says in an authoritative tone. "I strongly suggest we all do exactly as Murray just said. We don't want to add to the problem, right? So please promise me you'll both stay in your cabins until we reach the base, please? I know each of your parents; I'm responsible for you two, so please, promise me?"

The two young grad students answer in unison, "We promise, Dr. Marsh."

Chapter 21

A half an hour has passed, and Peter Marsh is once again sitting in front of his computer, but his attempts at writing are meager at best. It's impossible to focus his mind on anything other than the danger he knows is eminent. He's about to shut his system down when an instant message pops up on his screen; it was sent using the ship's intranet network: *Hey, it's Tom, I don't think we have much time, so be ready...* Marsh reads the message, then answers: *I'm ready, but how will we know when it's time?* Then Falcon types back: *You'll know...*

On the bridge, Moss has just ended a VHF radio call after a frustratingly protracted conversation with the American Naval Base at Subic Bay. The exchange began with an ensign lieutenant, then soon moved up the chain of command until Moss received an apologetic final word. He turns to Rafferty as he places the handset back in its cradle. "Bottom line, they don't want to get involved," Moss reports, as he attempts to mask his frustration. "They've informed me that under the circumstances, they aren't able to accommodate us... they said they'll lend assistance in the event of a natural disaster, but..."

"Same cover your ass bullshit..." Rafferty scowls.

"I should have seen this coming," Moss continues. "They don't know how to classify this event. They have no idea what's really going on out here, and they aren't about to follow the lead of the local authorities; that's just off the table. It's the chain of command, Razz, and we're not only a thousand steps down from the top, we're no longer on the ladder. You know the drill; they're not going to commit resources until they see this as a threat, and only after they know exactly what's going on, and only then after they get the green light from on high."

Rafferty looks down at the chart plotter now crowded with ships in distress. "So what's our next move?"

Moss is resolute, "We keep a level head, we keep moving south, and we stay prepared."

* * *

Alistair Fairchild had not always wanted to be a marine biologist. He'd come into the field somewhat accidentally, in fact; she was blond, willowy, smart, and Alistair fell for her hard, so much so that he switched his major from computer science to marine science in order that the two of them could share classes together. Then she took a summer internship at a prestigious whale research center, where the director took more than a passing interest in her. By the end of the summer they were engaged.

Alistair had considered returning to computers, but the subject no longer interested him as much as marine science. So he stuck with it. He eventually earned his under graduate degree, then his masters, then Alistair applied and was accepted as a doctoral candidate working under Dr. Peter Marsh, one of the world's leading authorities in the study of sharks. And although Alistair has immense respect for Dr. Marsh as an ichthyologist, he is not, as Alistair is now observing, a master of cyber security. Alistair watches as the typed exchange between Dr. Marsh and Dr. Falcon appears on his own computer. He's not quite sure what to make of it, but it's obvious they're up to something.

• • •

The first vibrations would not have been noticeable to anyone but Moss. As he stands on the bridge, he senses a slight hum coming up through the floor of the ninety-seven-meter-long ship. Yet, even for Moss, a man so intimately familiar with his vessel that something as innocuous as a new crew member coming on helm during a night watch for the first time could wake him from a sound sleep, this sensation was so marginal that it registered first in his subconscious. Moss waits a minute, maybe less… there it is again. He glances across the bridge toward Rafferty. "Did you feel that, Razz?" Rafferty looks up from the navigation screen.

"No, do you feel something, Ax?"

"Yeah, I do," Moss answers. "Alert the crew, I want everyone up top."

Down in the ship's expansive engine room, a glistening, spit and polished, state-of-the-art compartment housing two giant Caterpillar diesel power plants with a complement of four electric generators, an electronic alarm signals that one of the ship's two main propeller shafts isn't turning as it should. Its driveshaft is over torque for the amount of horsepower being sent. Pete, the ship's engineer, turns off the alarm, then checks the engine's telemetry on an electronic display. "It looks like the prop is fouled," he says to his assistant, Sam. "We gotta shut down engine one." He turns to Sam. "Call up to the bridge and tell 'em what's going on, will ya? It's probably another damn drift net; that shit's everywhere these days."

On the bridge, Rafferty receives the message from the engine room; he turns to Moss: "Pete says they just had an alarm on engine one; they think the prop's fouled on a net. They're shutting it down."

Moss exhales in disgust. "Just what we need. Tell him to keep engine two running at best speed. We can't afford to stop; we need to keep moving."

Rafferty relays the message, then turns back to see Moss looking down at the men assembling on deck. "Looks like your hunch was right; good call."

"Maybe," Moss answers, "but something tells me there's more than just a piece of fishnet down there. You and I better suit up."

Chapter 22

Peter Marsh is lying in his bunk when he senses the ship yaw slightly. He's felt this before; it happened when one of the ship's engines had to be shut down. Six months on board *Fearless* has given the veteran marine scientist his own feel for her personality. He sits up in his bunk as his intuition kicks in, and anxiety fills his gut. He gets ready to leave; something tells him he better get down to the lab.

On deck, eight fully armed crew pace their assigned areas. The seasoned mercenaries diligently patrol the ship's perimeter, yet so far at least, there's nothing all that unusual going on, just calm seas, a sunny tropical day, and one less engine.

Meanwhile, the interior of the ship is eerily quiet as Dr. Peter Marsh cautiously makes his way down the corridor leading to the main lab. He has just passed by the open door leading into the ship's media room when he hears voices further down the hallway. Marsh quickly doubles back, then steps inside. As Marsh stands motionless in a corner of the darkened room, he can hear a conversation between two crewmen as they pass the doorway.

"Pete says it's a net, but my gut tells me otherwise," one crew member says to the other.

"I wish your gut would tell you to stop eating those MRE's; your farts are disgusting, man."

Marsh can feel his heart rate go up as he watches the two armed men walk past the doorway. His palms are wet, his breathing is rapid and shallow; he feels embarrassed. *This is ridiculous…* Marsh thinks. *I would have made a terrible soldier…* The voices fade and once again the ship feels empty. Marsh steps from the corner of the media room. Moving past the overstuffed couches and low coffee tables, he aligns himself with the open door until he's able to peer outside the room and down the long, dimly lit corridor.

The main lab is only ten meters away. Marsh pulls his security keycard from his shirt pocket, takes a deep breath, then walks swiftly to the door. He hurriedly swipes the keycard through the sensor as he nervously glances in each direction. The lock softly beeps, then flashes green. Marsh turns the handle and walks inside the darkened lab. He gently holds back the heavy door to make sure it closes quietly, then Marsh turns to see Alistair sitting at the main computer display.

"What the hell are you doing here?"

"My job, Dr. Marsh. I'm your lab assistant, remember?"

Marsh reaches over and flips on the lights. "Well I should be upset, I guess, but you're here, so we might as well get to work." As Marsh walks toward the computer display, Alistair quickly shuts it down. Marsh reaches the desk Alistair is sitting behind; he's now standing opposite of where Alistair is seated, and behind the computer display. "So you felt the engine shut down too?" Marsh asks.

"Um… yeah, I sure did Dr. Marsh," Alistair says as he quietly pulls a USB flash drive from the computer, then slips it into his pocket. Along with the threat to the ship, Alistair recognizes the threat to the team's research, and he's not about to risk losing six months worth of work towards his doctorate; he's keeping a copy for himself.

Marsh steps behind the desk. "Why don't you fire up the sonar imaging system, Alistair. I think we should have a look at what's under the ship's hull."

Alistair springs from his chair, then strides over to the sonar imaging system's control panel. "So what do you think is down there, Dr. Marsh?"

"I hope nothing, but I think it's best we have a look." Marsh grabs the chair Alistair was using, rolls it up to the computer's flat screen display and then sits down. "As soon as it's running, Alistair, just send the live images over to this screen, ok? Oh… and make sure the unit's recording the feed."

"Sure, Dr. Marsh, I have it set to record. It's coming up now."

As the color sonar imaging system comes on line, Marsh leans in close to the display in order to study the output that's now being sent to him. "Well, there's a lot of clutter down there," Marsh observes. "Let's go ahead and widen the beam to max, shall we?"

Alistair makes the adjustment and then walks over to see for himself. "Whoa! Did you just see that?" Alistair points toward the outer edges of the live feed.

"No, I missed it," answers Marsh. "No, wait… what the devil is that?"

As the two men carefully watch the glowing screen in front of them, what appears to be the edge of a large mass becomes briefly visible, first passing on the starboard side, then to port. The object moves so rapidly, they're both forced to wait and watch several times before they are able to see the mass more clearly. Then it suddenly fills the screen as it moves directly beneath them. Marsh attempts to sharpen the image by weeding out interference using the computer; at that moment, the mass becomes more discernible.

"Maybe it's a really big school of sardines," Alistair suggests.

But Marsh knows otherwise; Alistair hasn't seen what he's just seen. "No, I don't think so; sardines aren't going to move this fast, even if they're being chased." Marsh continues to fine-tune the image, hoping to reveal more definition. Then the mass briefly splits in two, the momentary separation allows for the individual fish to become more visible. "My god it's them, it's the horde." Marsh looks up at Alistair. "Alistair, quick, roll back to that sequence and make me a set of printouts."

"Right away, Dr. Marsh."

Armed with the printouts, Marsh is much more confident as he now walks openly down the corridor, then up the two flights of stairs to the bridge, where he gets a couple of strange looks from crew members as he enters. Rafferty spots him first. "Dr. Marsh, we weren't expecting you; we're on a ship-wide security alert."

"Yes of course Mr. Rafferty. I apologize for my intrusion, but I have something you gentlemen need to see." Marsh lays the printouts on the chart table. "I've been running a sonar feed in the lab. There's a large mass moving directly underneath us; you'll want to see this."

Moss looks up. "Show me what you've got."

Marsh spreads the images out across the table as Moss and Rafferty look on. "I isolated these still images from the live feed; note the time sequence," Marsh explains.

As the two men examine the series of images, Moss notes the timing of each one as he quickly thumbs through them. "This thing is moving fast. Do you think it's them?"

Marsh points toward the last two images in the series, the ones that show the division point where the individuals become clearly visible, the one that shows the clear outlines of a large mass of mutilated sharks... "Yes Mr. Moss, I'm afraid I do."

Moss raises up from the chart table. "Thank you for this information, Dr. Marsh, but if you'll return to your cabin now, it would take one less concern off my list."

"Yes of course, sir, I'll go straight away."

Marsh leaves the bridge, and wastes no time getting back to his cabin, noting that crewmen seem to be watching to make sure he does just that. Once inside, he flips on his computer; a message sent from Falcon is waiting for him: *Ok Peter, what have you been up to then? Spill it...*

Marsh quickly types out a response: *I was in the lab, ran the sonar, the horde is here, no doubt they're somehow fouling the prop, they're directly under the ship: confirmed.*

Thirty seconds go by before Falcon messages back, *Good work, you informed Moss of course?*

Marsh exhales nervously as he types his response, *Yes, I'm certain they are now moving to full battle stations.*

As Marsh finishes, he leans back in his chair. The cursor at the bottom of the screen blinks silently for a few moments, then Falcon responds: *It's time.*

Chapter 23

The alarm coming from engine two's control panel sends Pete, the ship's engineer, over the edge. He's been steadily working to free-up engine one's fouled prop since being forced to take it offline an hour ago; running it at low RPM, then brief spurts in reverse, in an attempt to loosen whatever is wrapped around it. At times his technique has worked, thus the frustration. As Pete carefully nurses his mechanical patient along, engine one's screw begins spinning freely again; buoying the seasoned engineer's spirits as he is able to gradually increase power.

Twice he's managed to get the unit fully online and running cleanly at normal RPM, but then, after an encouraging ten-minute run, the prop fouls again. It's infuriating; it makes no sense. So when the alarm on engine two suddenly goes off, so does Pete. As the electronic alarm beeps incessantly, Pete runs over to silence the annoyance. Then he sees the worrisome row of red-line outputs on engine two's display, and begins cursing loudly. Reluctantly, he proceeds to shut down what was his ship's remaining engine. "Goddamn-mother-fucking-shit!" Pete shouts as Sam, his assistant engineer, cowers. Then Pete catches himself. "Sorry for that, Sam. I'm gonna keep working here. Call up to the bridge, let him know what's going on. They're gonna be plenty upset with the both of us."

"Dammit," Rafferty angrily slams the com's receiver back in its cradle. "We're dead in the water."

* * *

Down in his cabin, Falcon quickly types another message to Marsh: *Looks like I got back just in time, are you ready?* Just as Falcon hits send, a slight shudder resonates through the ship's hull. Falcon freezes momentarily, but then the ship goes silent again as Marsh's response appears on his screen: *I can't do this Tom, I'm sorry...*

Inside his own cabin, Marsh waits nervously for his friend's answer; he feels like a complete shit. He's afraid, he's angry, he pushes his chair back from his desk in disgust just as Falcon bursts in.

Marsh turns to see Falcon, "Tom... how did you..."

In one stride Falcon is in Marsh's face as he grabs his shirt collar with both hands. "You damn well will do this, Peter. You know what's at stake here; we have no choice!" Falcons eyes flip intensely back and forth as he stares down a terrified Marsh.

"Tom!" Marsh pleads. "I'm sorry, I'm no good at this sort of thing. I'm not like you; I never have been!"

At that point Falcon slaps Marsh hard across his face. Marsh is completely caught off guard. At first he's stunned, then he's angry. He shoves Falcon back against the desk, then gets to his feet just as Falcon is coming at him again. At that moment Marsh clocks him, landing a perfectly placed right punch squarely against Falcon's left cheekbone. Falcon staggers back, holding his jaw as the shock and pain rattle through his head,

"Shit," Falcon rasps. "That was a good punch, my friend."

Marsh looks down at his tightly clenched and throbbing right fist.

"You wanna hit me again?" taunts Falcon, "Come on, you know you do."

Marsh lifts his fists; he's fully prepared to strike. "This shit is all your fault, you caused this. I don't owe you…"

"You're right, Peter, it is all my fault," Falcon says in between breaths. "And you don't owe me a fucking thing. But you're no piker, you're no goddam piker, and I can't do this without you. We had an agreement, and if you let me down, a lot more people will die, I guarantee you that."

Falcon can see the adrenaline pumping through Marsh; it's building like a boiler. "You feel that? You feel that energy running you? That's not fear, my friend, that's your survival tool, that's what's going to get you through this, you hear me?"

* * *

On deck, the crew can only watch as the wake left behind by *Fearless* slowly fades and the ninety-seven-meter-long ship begins to drift. A dark green ridge-line of jungle-covered mountains is visible four miles off their port side. The mood is tense as the men steadily walk their designated patrol patterns. Distributed bow to stern, two men are positioned on the helipad just behind the ship's prow. A few meters behind the chopper pad is the tender bay, where two more men walk alongside the two massive hydraulic hatches beneath which the tenders and service vehicles are stored below deck. This is also where the helicopter itself would be stored, if it was on board.

Up at her highest point looms the broad forward bay of windows that marks the bridge, and directly beneath the bridge lies the main superstructure, where two more men are positioned on each side. On the backside of the superstructure, between her satellite communications, radar array, and the exhaust stacks, lies a narrow walk-through, a passageway running the beam of the ship. It's just in front of the submarine launch platform at the stern, where two more men currently patrol.

A crewman rounds the corner, after walking the port side of the stern's outer perimeter. He passes by the hydraulic crane used to launch and retrieve the mini-sub. As the crewman reaches the port entrance of the passageway, something registers from the corner of his eye. He turns to look just as a large zombie bull shark lunges at him. Instinctively the crewman lets loose a brief burst from his MP5. Three of the rounds explode into their target as they rip through the shark's rotted flesh, sending bits of it slinging up across the outer bulkhead. The bull shark's rabid jaws are still snapping however as it lunges again. The crewman blasts another six rounds into the zombie, blowing the shark's lower jaw to bits. Then he takes a step back, coolly observing the now-motionless zombie shark lying in bits at his feet. His weapon still raised, he hears his radio light up:

"Shots fired! We have shots fired!"

Moss cuts in: "Hold your positions. Who fired those shots? Report."

The crewman calmly pulls his radio from his belt. "Chief, It's Mike. I've just encountered a large shark on deck. I'm at the port entrance to the aft passageway; target disabled."

"On my way," answers Moss.

As Mike studies the splattered remains of the bull shark, something hits his right leg from behind. The force of impact violently throws him off his feet and knocks his weapon from his hands. The fall lands him face first into the shark's long-dead corpse. It's rotten, odor-laced gelatinous outer flesh squirts up into his mouth and nose. As Mike scrambles to push himself away from the bull shark's putrid remains, he realizes he's being dragged across the deck; something has hold of him, and it's got him good.

Mike groans as what feels like a dozen jagged knives cut deep into his flesh. Through sheer force of will, he grabs for his weapon and just manages to catch the edge of the MP5's shoulder strap as it's being pulled away from his body. With his weapon now back in his hands, Mike cries out in agony as he leverages himself against the grip of the shark that now has his right leg tightly between its jaws. He rolls upright, aims, and squeezes the trigger. A volley of rounds fire into the morbid flesh of the massive zombie tiger shark. Her grip remains firm, however, as she goes back over the side, taking Mike with her.

Chapter 24

Moss runs flat out with two crew members in tow. He chose the shortest route to the aft passageway, an interior maintenance access corridor that runs the length of the ship. Its path takes Moss past the engine room, water makers, and the sewage treatment facility, along with the ship's heating, air-conditioning, and electrical systems room. Moss can cover the distance from the bridge in well under a minute. After the three men top the stairway that leads to a storage area located under the communications array, they hear a third round of shots go off. Moss knows they're coming from Mike's location. Once they reach the storage area, it's a brief sprint to a hatch leading outside and into the passageway. As Moss pushes open the exterior hatch, he immediately encounters the remains of the large bull shark that was taken out by Mike. Moss grabs his radio: "Mike, come in Mike, do you read?" Then one of the two crewmen notices the blood trail.

"Chief, over here."

Moss kneels down to examine the broad swath of fresh blood smeared across the deck. The path leads up and over the railing. The two crewmen rush to the side, where they frantically search the calm water below, but there's no sign of their lost man. Alex

Moss' first reaction is anger... anger at the senseless loss of a good man, as an all too familiar torrent of emotion boils up through his body. It's a feeling he'd long hoped he would never have to experience ever again in his life, but here it is, slicing open the old wounds once again. Then a second wave of anger rushes in. This one is directed inward, as he feels the weight of responsibility for a man's death crashing down hard on his shoulders. Then he stops himself; he can't grieve now, it's not the time. Moss freely allows his training and experience to take over as he pushes his personal feelings aside; there's work to do. Moss stands, then picks up his radio. "All crew on deck fall back immediately; I want everyone back inside now."

The rest of the men take Mike's loss bitterly but silently. A twice decorated veteran of the first Gulf War, he was one of the oldest members of the crew. He was also a man they highly respected, but nobody was blaming Moss for his death. Putting up a secure perimeter is standard protocol when the ship is under threat of attack. It's a proven technique they'd successfully deployed in other high-risk locations such as certain areas of the Red Sea, the Andaman Sea, and parts of the Indian Ocean.

But this time the threat wasn't human, a factor the crew initially took somewhat lightly as they figured a bunch of rabid, re-animated fish should be easier to take down than a fleet of a dozen go-fast boats loaded with heavily armed, and desperate, pirates. Sure, they'd reasoned, the beach resort, cruise ship attack, even the infamous freezer ambush that went down just hours before had been horrific, but they were instigated against defenseless civilians, not expertly trained, seasoned, and well-armed mercenaries like themselves. In the aftermath of Mike's loss, however, they were all rapidly changing their opinions.

With all personnel back inside and all exterior hatches secured, Moss stands once more on the bridge, gazing out the front windows at a sea that seems to be turning against him. "I'm not going to have my guys picked off one by one by a bunch of goddamn fish," Moss complains. "Razz, any word from Pete on the engines?"

"He's working on it," Rafferty answers, "but he says whatever is fouling the props is getting worse. He hasn't been able to make any headway, but he's not giving up. The wind's building back in; it's starting to push us toward shore, but we aren't in any danger just yet..." As Rafferty speaks, something hits the ship's hull, sending a shudder up through the floor. Razz looks over at Moss: "What the hell was that?"

"It's them," observes Moss. "If I didn't know better, I'd say they were following a plan. It's like they're trying to smoke us out; it's what I would do." As Moss continues to scan the expanse of empty ocean in front of him, he notices a disturbance just off *Fearless'* starboard bow.

"Razz, check this out."

Rafferty and five crewmen move toward the windows; they can all see a strange upwelling that appears to be rising from far below. "It looks like the kind of burst you get when the sub is about to surface," one of the crew members observes.

"Yeah," adds Rafferty, "but this one's much bigger, and I don't think it's the Navy..."

* * *

Down in the darkened aft storage bay, Marsh and Falcon are making their move. They navigate cautiously in between crates containing spare parts, a rack of fishing gear, an assortment of mountain bikes and surfboards that belong to the crew, and a large

149

collection of various tools, when Marsh spots the hatchway he's been searching for. "Here's the hatch that leads outside,"

Falcon is just behind him. "Moss has ordered everyone inside. This is our perfect chance." As the two scientists are about to open the hatch, Falcon pauses. He stares intensely at Marsh. "This is a straightforward operation, Peter; there's nobody out there. We get outside, the sub is only a few meters away; you operate the crane, I drive the sub. Once you release the sub in the water, you run like hell back inside. You got me? It's easy-peasy, mon."

"Right," answers a nervous Marsh. "Easy-peasy."

The two men push open the hatch, run outside, and immediately, both of them nearly trip over the remains of the bull shark. "Oh dear god..." gasps Marsh as he encounters the broad swath of blood smeared across the deck.

"Run man, run!" Falcon shouts as he sprints for the mini-sub.

Marsh climbs the steel ladder leading to the crane's controls, while Falcon begins the process of releasing the mini-sub from her docking bay. As Marsh powers up the hydraulic crane, he watches Falcon deftly unlock the sub's release clamps, then her main access hatch. *How did you get those keys?* Marsh thinks to himself, then he's surprised as Falcon suddenly turns and winks at him. With the sub free of her restraints and her hatch open, Falcon quickly climbs inside the three-man sub.

On the bridge, Moss, Rafferty, and the other crewmen grow increasingly alarmed as the violently churning upwell now surging off the ship's bow rapidly expands. Moss turns to Razz: "Send out a ship-wide alert, tell everyone to brace now." Rafferty grabs the ship's comm and relays the order just as the sea in front of them explodes. The crew of *Fearless* watch with shared, mystified shock as a gigantic, roaring geyser expels an overwhelming horde of zombie sharks onto their ship. The men struggle against disbelief as the resulting raging tsunami of thousands of rotting shark corpses rushes straight at them from the forward deck.

The roar of the exploding wave grabs Peter Marsh's attention first. From his vantage point atop the hydraulic crane, he turns to see a wall of sharks rise above the bow of the ship, a sight that sends ice cold fear flowing down his spine. He turns back to see Falcon buckling himself inside the mini-sub. Marsh has just managed to successfully attach the lift cable, but every instinct now screams that there is no time; this isn't going to work. Marsh looks back toward the wave; it is huge, dark, and heading straight for them. It's moving fast, it rapidly overtakes the bow of the ship three hundred feet away; Marsh knows he's seen this wave before.

Every cell in his body tells him to run, but instead, Marsh frantically signals to Falcon, who is inside the acrylic-domed mini-sub. As Marsh waves his arms, Falcon looks up in confusion, but then he too spots the fast-approaching wave. Falcon instantly realizes they have to abort. He rips off his harness, then scrambles back out of the mini-sub just as Marsh is sliding down the ladder toward the deck. Falcon closes the sub's hatch behind him, then leaps from the platform to the deck below where Marsh is waiting for him.

The two men sprint for the narrow passageway just as the raging torrent of zombie sharks reaches the ship's aft section. As the horde washes over the aft deck, it hits the mini-sub. The force lifts the vehicle from its platform. The attached cable is now the only thing preventing the sub from being lost overboard as it dangles like a fish on a line straining against the arm of the crane. Broad daylight is instantly extinguished as the zombie horde blankets the ship.

The sea has now expelled its horde of living death, as if the ocean itself was attempting to exorcise the evil it has been forced to harbor. The reanimated corpses of long-dead sharks flow past the narrow opening in front of the passageway where Marsh and Falcon have taken shelter. While the turbulence caused by the wave pushes *Fearless* dramatically to port, the motion knocks Marsh off his feet. Falcon grabs Marsh by the arm, then drags him toward the exterior hatch just as zombie sharks begin to flood the passageway.

Falcon flings open the hatchway as the sharks race toward the two men. Hundreds of crazed, snapping jaws rapidly close in. Falcon shoves Marsh through the opening just as the deadly zombies reach the back of the hatchway. Falcon feels the incredible force of their bodies as they begin to pile against the outside of the door. He momentarily attempts to push against the enormous inertia, but it's impossible. Reflexively, he jumps as he grips the hatchway's inner handle, and the force slams the hatch shut. Once inside, Falcon falls to the floor, exhausted, while Marsh rushes to grab the handle and secure the hatch.

On the bridge, Moss, Rafferty, and five crew members are forced to watch as a liquid purgatory of rotted, reanimated fish violates their ship. As *Fearless* drifts helplessly, the grotesque horde ravages her forward deck, then thrusts against her white superstructure. Her crew look on with enraged disgust; then the first shark strikes the heavy front windows they are all standing behind. The men reflexively flinch as a second zombie shark smashes into the hurricane-rated glass that shields them from the deadly horde.

"Grab everything useful you can carry," Moss orders as more sharks begin to strike the windows. "Evacuate the bridge now." Moss, Rafferty, and the crewmen quickly grab armloads of gear.

They scoop up portable computer devices, several portable radios, handheld EPIRBs, and satellite phones.

Moss goes for the holstered Kukri blades and the weapons zipped inside the gear bag he'd left under the chart table just as a loud crack rifles through his ears. The men see that one of the windows has shattered; the glass is now held in place only by its reinforced laminate. "Out!" Moss shouts. "I want everyone out now!" As the men evacuate, Moss is the last to leave. As he shuts the steel door behind him, he knows he's just lost his command center. The rude knowledge that the sharks have won the opening battle infuriates him. Consumed with rage, Moss listens to the horde crash through the windows and fill his bridge.

Chapter 25

The sudden and unexpected evacuation from the bridge has caught Alex Moss off guard. The aftermath has left him dazed. The bridge is his base; it's an extension of himself, and the center of his world. As he reels from the loss, he feels uncertainty creeping in, a feeling he is very much unaccustomed to. Moss tries to fight back against the shock and confusion; he can't allow himself to succumb to emotion. He tries to clear his head, to focus on what needs to be done to insure the safety of his ship and the survival of his crew. "Guys, bring up the welding rig," Moss orders as he examines the door to the bridge. "We need this door secured; it has to be welded shut." Moss then turns to Razz. "Take a team; we need to inspect all of the windows, every cabin port. we have to find a way to secure everything."

Malcolm Rafferty, himself deeply shaken by what has just happened, is nonetheless bewildered by his friend's demand. "Ax, we don't have the materials or the time to weld over every opening," Rafferty says calmly as he evaluates the emotional state of his friend. "I suggest we regroup to the interior as quickly as possible. The hatchways are reinforced and watertight; they'll hold."

Moss listens carefully to Rafferty's suggestion. "You're right, Razz, I agree; we regroup down below. We need to gather the civilians."

"I'll take the guys with me; we'll handle it." Then Rafferty looks Moss in the eye. "You did the right thing back there."

Rafferty grabs an MP5 and the two P90s along with some extra clips from the gear bag lying at Moss' feet. He then signals for the men to follow him down below. Moss watches the men leave. Then he leans back against the door to his bridge and loudly exhales. From the other side of the reinforced door, he can still hear them. He reckons there must be dozens in there by now, and they're trashing the place. Not only are the sharks destroying hundreds of thousands of dollars in state-of–the-art navigational equipment and electronics, but his log books and all of his charts. Moss can hear them destroy everything as the horde wrecks the past four years of his life. In a rage he spins around, driving his fist into the steel door: "Mother-fucking sharks!"

• • •

Falcon is sitting on the floor of the aft storage bay as he tries to catch his breath. "Are you all right, Peter?"

Marsh braces himself against a wall rack stacked with mountain bikes as he recovers. "Yeah, I think so," Marsh answers as he checks himself for injuries. "I'm fine, no worries. How about you?"

Falcon smiles back at Marsh. "Given the circumstances, I'd say I'm in remarkable shape."

"So, old friend, what the hell do we do now?"

Falcon glances up at Marsh, his voice shifting in tone. "We wait right here for our next chance, and we try again."

"Are you totally insane?" Marsh says as he pushes himself upright. "You did see those sharks out there, right?"

"We'll get another chance, Peter, I know we will, and this time it has to work."

* * *

Rafferty and his team move swiftly down a corridor as they bang on the doors of the civilian crew cabins: "Emergency evacuation!" they shout as they quickly gather together civilian staff who'd previously been told to wait in their quarters. Then Murray approaches Rafferty.

"We can't locate the fish docs. Neither one of them is in their cabins."

Rafferty quickly searches the group of civilians, and he spots Alistair. "Alistair, have you seen Dr. Marsh or Dr. Falcon?

"Not for over an hour," Alistair answers. "Maybe they're in one of the labs?"

Rafferty turns back to Murray. "Take Dan and Rich; go check the labs."

"Right," Murray answers. He spins around, then quickly disappears down the corridor with the two crewmen close behind him.

As Rafferty turns back to the group, he spots Moss walking toward him. "We've got this, Ax. We're almost finished here. I have the rest of the crew setting up a shelter down below in the service corridor. They're stocking blankets, food, water and medical supplies," he says as he looks at Moss. "How are you doing?"

"I'm fine, good work," Moss answers. "What's this about Dr. Marsh and Dr. Falcon? Are they missing?"

"They weren't in their cabins," Rafferty answers. "I have Murray, Rich, and Dan checking the labs, but if they're not there I'm not sure what we can do."

Moss looks at Rafferty. "Nobody goes outside to look for them under any circumstances. If those two went outside, they're on their own as far as I'm concerned."

Murray, Rich, and Dan arrive at the first of the ship's two research labs. Murray quickly pulls out his security card and opens the door, but the three men find the lab dark, silent, and empty. "Ok then, nothing here," announces the frustrated Australian. They then sprint for the stairway leading to the main lab located one deck below. Dan is in front as they start down the stairwell, the group is moving at high speed when they nearly run over a zombie shark.

It was once a magnificent silver-tip, but in its reanimated zombie state, the shark is now a mutilated corpse reeking of death. As the men lurch backwards, Rich swings his P90 into firing position as the shark lunges with its jaws open. Then Murray fires his Taser. The electrodes hit their mark; the zombie silver-tip convulses, then collapses in a heap, while a thick gray ooze begins to pour from its mouth. Murray calmly reaches toward Rich and places his hand on the muzzle of the P90 Rich still tightly grips, then gently pushes the muzzle toward the floor. "There now, you see that? You don't always need guns, mate."

Chapter 26

Rafferty supervises as eight civilian staff and the remainder of the science team are ushered down below to the makeshift shelter located in the maintenance corridor.

"How long do we need to stay down here, Mr. Rafferty?" Alistair asks,

"To be honest, kid, we're improvising," Rafferty hurriedly answers. "I really can't say. We're just trying to keep anyone else from getting hurt. If we know you guys are safe down here, it's a lot easier for us to do our job. You understand, right?"

"Yeah, I guess I do," answers Alistair. "Thanks for looking out for us... uh... can I ask you something?

"Make it quick. I'm busy."

"You saw them, right? You saw the sharks?"

"I wish I hadn't," answers Rafferty. "Let's just leave it at that." Rafferty's radio suddenly crackles with static, he grabs it off his belt: "Repeat the message; I'm in a bad area."

Then Rafferty hears Murray's voice break through briefly: "We encountered... stairwell... Taser worked."

"On my way." Rafferty quickly glances back at Alistair. "Alistair, help me out; make sure everyone gets settled, ok?"

"Sure Mr. Rafferty, you got it."

Heading back up, Rafferty crosses paths with a fully armed Moss and four equally well-armed crewmen. "I just heard a radio transmission from Murray…"

"So did I," adds Moss. "They came across a shark in the aft stairwell, near the main lab. We're heading there now."

Down in the stairwell, Murray holsters his Taser as he examines the now de-animated shark remains. "Look what we have here, fellas. Once these zombies are back to being dead they're not that scary anymore, are they." He turns toward Rich and Dan. "You guys go ahead and check the main lab and then come right back. I'll wait here; the Chief's on his way." The two men gingerly step over the dead shark and then move rapidly down the rest of the stairwell toward the lab just as Moss, Rafferty, and the four crewmen arrive at the scene.

"So the Taser did work," observes Moss.

The group gaze curiously down at the badly decomposed shark, as a puddle of ooze around the corpse slowly drips down through the stairway's metal grating.

"Jeez, that thing stinks!" remarks one of the crew.

Murray holds his Taser up in front of Moss. "It worked great, Chief. One shot and the ugly sod was done for; everyone should have one of these." A sudden rumble from below sends a shudder through the ship's hull. The men all reach for something solid as *Fearless* briefly shifts to port, then rights herself.

Moss looks at Rafferty. "They're trying to get through the…" shots ring out; the sounds cut Moss off mid-sentence.

"Downstairs!" shouts Rafferty as he reaches for his radio. "Dan, Rich, come in."

Dan answers Rafferty: "We're outside the lab; we're cut off!" Then the ship fills once more with the high-pitched trill of rapid automatic weapons fire emanating from the P90s Rich and Dan each carry.

"On our way," ends Rafferty as Moss leaps over the dead shark and sprints down the stairs with the rest of the men close behind him. Once in the corridor, Moss can see his crewmen; they're pinned against the wall just outside the lab with three zombie sharks snapping at them rabidly. Dan quickly acknowledges Moss, Rafferty, and the crewmen, then turns back and fires at the sharks in front of him. The percussion of the live rounds echoes painfully in everyone's ears.

Murray steps forward, then carefully aims his Taser. "Right… enough of that racket." He fires, and takes out one of the sharks instantly. Then a second crewman steps up beside Murray as he aims his own Taser. Meanwhile Dan and Rich continue to pump bullets into the two remaining zombie sharks. A second set of electrodes hit their target and efficiently dispatch a second shark, while the third is finally destroyed by Dan and Rich at the cost of everyone's ears and dozens of rounds of ammunition; Moss has seen the light.

• • •

Marsh and Falcon listen as the din of submachine gunfire rings through the ship. "What's happening?" exclaims Marsh. "What should we do? We have to do something, don't we?"

"We can't help them," Falcon answers calmly. "They're highly trained mercenaries; they know what they're doing." Then the ship shifts once more as a low rumble vibrates up through the floor of the storage bay. Unfazed, Falcon continues: "We have our own job to focus on; our next opportunity is coming."

* * *

Down in the cramped maintenance corridor, Alistair, two armed crewmen, and the rest of the civilian staff brace nervously as loud rumbles now repeatedly rise up through the hull. The sounds are strong enough to cancel out the brief bursts of distant gunfire. As the ship rolls from side to side, Alistair suddenly stands and begins to push his way toward the exit, when Brian attempts to stop him.

"Where are you going?" Brian asks,

"We have to get out of here," Alistair answers. "We have to get out now." Alistair shoves Brian out of the way, he then continues down the narrow corridor until he reaches the two crewmen currently standing watch.

As Alistair looks up at the two men, they both smile. "Ok, go ahead," says one of the two men. "We won't stand in your way, will we, Seth?"

"Not me, Cal," Seth answers sarcastically. "If Alistair here wants out of the safe zone we've carefully set up for him, then be my guest, but don't expect me to go out there and patch you up; the medical kit stays right here with me."

Cal then makes direct eye contact with Alistair. "I don't know about you, Seth, but I'd rather put up with a little noise than run into more of those damn sharks,"

"You got that right," adds Seth, as he too stares down at Alistair. "But then again, you've got your stun baton, right? So you'll be fine once you get out there; I think you can handle it."

Alistair suddenly looks down at his belt. "Oh, um, I'm not sure what happened to the baton; I don't have it anymore." Seth and Cal both smirk sarcastically as Alistair silently turns around and walks back to where he'd been previously sitting.

* * *

In the aftermath of the shark shoot-out near the main lab, Moss first sees to Dan and Rich. "You guys ok? Any injuries?"

The two men briefly glance down at themselves and then each other, recognizing that wounds taken during battle can sometimes go unnoticed until after it's over. "No, Chief," answers Dan, "we're good to go."

"No sign of the fish docs either," adds Rich.

On hearing that piece of news, Moss sighs as another crewman approaches. "Chief, sorry to make your day worse, but you better have a look at this." The crewman hands Moss a small tablet computer; it shows the ship's current location. Moss looks down at the display. His jaw visibly tightens as he processes what it tells him, then he hands it to Rafferty.

"Shit…" Razz whispers under his breath as he studies the electronic navigational chart displayed on the screen. The tablet computer is tapped into the ship's network and displays the position of *Fearless* in real time. It shows that she's now drifting dangerously close to shore.

Chapter 27

Even without access to the bridge, Moss would be able to helm *Fearless* to safety remotely using the same small tablet he now holds in his hands. That is, if the engines were operational. She's a sophisticated vessel, and during her construction *Fearless* was fitted with several anti-pirate features such as the reinforced, bulletproof steel door to the bridge, multiple radar systems, including FLIR—forward looking infrared—night vision, and the ability to command her remotely from any part of the vessel using the touchpad. But only if the engines are on line, of course. Moss stares at the tablet. "What's the latest from Pete? Any progress at all?"

"I just had two of the guys down there checking up on him," answers Rafferty. "He's working nonstop, but he says whatever is clogging up the screws is doing a hell of a job. Other than that, the engines themselves are fully operational, so he wants to keep at it."

"We know what's down there," adds Moss, "and something tells me they're not going to just give up and go away." As Moss speaks, another low-pitched rumble runs up through the hull; yet, this time, nobody reacts.

* * *

Peter Marsh curiously observes as Falcon rummages through the various crates and boxes stored in the aft compartment they are currently holed up inside. Falcon busily opens two large tool boxes, then sorts through an assortment of sports gear that had been left in the storage bay by the crew. "So what exactly are you looking for?" Marsh finally inquires.

"Anything useful," Falcon answers, "anything that might be effective against those beasties out there."

"That's it," announces an exasperated Marsh, "you sir, are officially a nutter." Marsh stands, then walks over to where Falcon has been pulling items from a crate he's opened. "Ok then, I'll bite," Marsh inquires. "What have you got there?"

Falcon briefly pauses, then he looks up at Marsh from the box he's just opened. "Ha ha," he answers sarcastically, "is that supposed to be funny then?

"No Tom," answers Marsh, "of course not... however, as you have so often pointed out: levity is a proven stress reducer... it's just that, I don't see the point of all this. Perhaps we should just look for some cards, and enjoy a few rounds of poker while we wait for the next wave of the zombie shark apocalypse, what do you say, old friend?"

"Personally, I prefer productive work," Falcon answers curtly. "Here, give me a hand with this." Marsh watches as Falcon heaves against the heavy latch of a large commercial tool case.

"Hold on," Marsh interrupts. "I've seen one of these before. Allow me..." Marsh reaches in; he turns the latch in the opposite direction, and the case easily pops open. Inside is a portable welding kit. Marsh sees the contents of the case. "Oh right, now that looks like something we can use."

"Most certainly does," answers Falcon. "This is going into the arsenal." Falcon closes the case. He looks briefly at Marsh, then hurriedly begins to gesture around the room like a man strung out on stress, caffeine, lack of nicotine, and overwhelming guilt; which is, in fact, who he is. "Along that far wall, I found some fire extinguishers, and over here we have industrial cleaning supplies, and over on the work bench I found a soldering set and a can of acetone, and over in that corner over there are a few expired dive tanks and..."

"What the bloody hell are you babbling on about?" Marsh is clearly exasperated. "What are we? MacGyver? Do you honestly believe we can defeat thousands of zombie sharks with some industrial tools, a bunch of homemade chemical weapons, and a few improvised pyrotechnics? I'm sorry but that's just looney."

"Peter, we're scientists! We can do this!"

"Yes of course," quips Marsh. Then he looks Falcon in the eye. "We're shark biologists, Tom, we're PhD Ichthyologists, we're not chemists or engineers. We're the *fish doctors*, Tom." Marsh glances at the rack of fishing gear he's standing next to. "We might as well take the simple direct approach." Marsh reaches over, pulls a large rod and reel from its storage rack, then mockingly pretends to reel one in. "Come to papa, you sons of bitches."

Falcon suddenly stands up straight. "Peter, that's it! we're the fish doctors!" Falcon walks over to a small backpack hanging from the handlebars of a mountain bike while Marsh returns the fishing rod to its storage rack, then follows him. "Right," Falcon directs as he looks at Marsh, "point taken, my friend. That whole bit was a stupid idea, cross it out—forget it. The answer's been here under our noses the whole time."

Falcon reaches into the backpack and pulls out the Taser. "We'll use this." He holds the Taser up in front of Marsh. "It's amazing, but when that Murray chap first handed us these, I thought it was some sort of joke, you know? Just something to make us feel better. But then I got to thinking that if we ran into these Neanderthals while we were trying to get to the sub, we could use the Taser to incapacitate them. It never occurred to me that this thing would be effective against the sharks themselves. But we know it's an energy field that gives them their mobility. Theoretically, a sufficiently powerful electrical charge, like one from this Taser, should short it out. Peter, this might be all we need to disrupt their bond with the talisman."

Marsh smiles. "We'll be needing more than one then," he pulls his own Taser out from where he had it stuffed under the back of his belt. "I was thinking the same as you, actually. Now I feel like a complete idiot, really. I never thought to use it back there on deck, you know?"

"Hey mate, I just now thought of it myself, so if two stun guns are good, then this should be even better," Falcon pulls a stun baton out of the pack.

"How did you get that?" Marsh knows he shouldn't be surprised, but he's still impressed.

"I nicked it when Alistair wasn't looking."

"Good work!" chuckles Marsh. "Those reanimated elasmobranchs don't stand a chance against a couple of boffin fish doctors after all."

* * *

By midday, intense tropical heat has raised the temperature inside *Fearless* to an uncomfortable level. Beads of sweat rise on the brows of Moss and his crew as they attempt to come up with a strategy to safely evacuate the civilians off the ship before she strikes the reef. Although the ship's four generators are currently fully operational, Moss has Pete running just two of them in order to conserve fuel. So the air conditioning is only on in key sections, such as the room housing the computer network. Meanwhile, the onshore sea breeze continues to slowly push *Fearless* ever closer toward the rocky shoreline. She's starting to drift into more shallow water as the jungle-covered mountains that were once distant on the horizon, now loom high overhead.

"We could use the lifeboats," Rafferty suggests, "evacuate the civilians to shore. The lifeboats are completely enclosed, they're tough; they should be able to make it."

"I'm not willing to take that chance," answers Moss. "You saw what they did to that beach resort. These things have the ability to follow the lifeboats right up onto shore. Land doesn't seem to stop them."

Then a crewman steps forward, the same crewman who handed Moss the tablet just minutes before. "Chief, I have an idea."

"Steve, let's hear it," answers Moss.

"We could use explosives. I could rig them with a delay; it would be like a depth charge. We clear these things out, then we launch the lifeboats."

"It's a good suggestion," answers Moss, "but they are too close to the ship, and as we've been drifting toward shore, we've also been losing depth. Unfortunately, we're in shallow water now; any explosives we set off will probably sink us." Moss sighs once more. He knows there has to be a way to get people safely off the ship, and he knows they have to find the solution on their own, as no outside help will be coming. Then Moss hears his radio.

"*Fearless, Fearless, Fearless*, this is GlobalRanger, over."

Rafferty and the crewmen all quickly close in tightly around Moss, hoping against hope that the voice they thought they just heard is actually real. Moss snaps the radio from his belt. "GlobalRanger, this is *Fearless*. Flip, is that you?"

"Chief, sorry for the holdup. I wanted to get there sooner; I got your message. Getting this bird out of hock took longer than expected."

At that moment cheers rise up from the group of men surrounding Moss, as Steve, Rafferty, and the rest of the men hug and high-five each other. A smile actually appears on Moss' face as he answers, "Flip, I don't know if you just heard that, but your voice is the best news we've had all day. What's your ETA?"

"Yeah, I heard, Chief. No worries, cavalry's on its way; ETA in thirty minutes."

Chapter 28

John Halpern is from Geelong, Australia, and he flew his first airplane at age fourteen. He later entered the Australian army, where he became a helicopter pilot. After primary training, he was recruited into SASR, Australia's elite Special Air Service Regiment. As a member of the 171st Aviation Squadron, he flew Sikorsky S-70 Blackhawks. His first combat deployment overseas came as part of ISAF, the international security assistance force in Afghanistan, where he would fly hundreds of sorties.

It was during a night mission into the Hindu Kush mountains northeast of Kabul that the Blackhawk he was flying started taking fire from the ground. In an attempt to avoid a MANPAD surface-to-air missile, John performed a perfect barrel roll with his Blackhawk. The unorthodox maneuver was successful, hence the name *Flip*. Which is exactly what happened to the team inside John's chopper, Alex Moss being among them. The two men have been friends ever since. So when Moss needed a helicopter pilot for the project he was overseeing in Germany, Flip was his first choice.

The Bell 429 had been personally selected by Flip. With excellent range and room for seven plus pilot, she'd been a workhorse, but even a workhorse needs time off. The Bell has been in

Manila undergoing scheduled maintenance. However, the parts Flip ordered got held up in Philippine customs. He and Moss spent two weeks clearing up the paperwork, using up hours of satellite phone time in the process. With the parts finally in hand, Flip was in the process of putting the Bell back together when he got word from Moss that *Fearless* was under threat.

Just as he was ready to fly again, however, Flip got the other bad news. The fixed-base operator (FBO) that was operating out of the hanger he was using went bankrupt. The bank holding the paper had the police impound all of the aircraft inside the hanger until clear title could be proven. Getting the Bell "out of hock" wasted another day. But now that she was finally back in the air, Flip was wasting no time flying to the aid of his friends.

* * *

With Rich and Dan's help, Murray quickly gathers the rest of the Tasers and stun weapons from the ship's hidden compartment. "There you are, you little nippers," Murray crows, pulling crates filled with XREP cartridges from a shelf; then he turns toward Rich and Dan: "Make sure you guys grab all those Herstal SLP's too," he directs. The men hurriedly fill several duffle bags with the cartridges, the rest of the stun batons, the twelve-gauge tactical shotguns, and the remaining Tasers.

Swinging a heavy bag up onto each shoulder, Murray flashes a wry smile back at Rich and Dan. "What do ya say we go fry up some fish and chips?" With less than twenty minutes until Flip's arrival, Moss and Rafferty quickly gather their team together. "Gentlemen, we just got the best break we've had all day," Moss announces. "Flip's on his way, and we have to make the most of this opportunity." As Moss speaks, he can clearly see the elevated mood of the men standing in front of him. "We also have another piece of positive news, and it's these Tasers." Moss holds a Taser high as he speaks.

"Thanks to Murray, we know a hit from a stun weapon is the quickest, most efficient way to take these things out. Murray, Rich, and Dan have refreshed our supplies; the bag's are over there against the wall, so everybody will be able to stock up. Ok, moving forward, our plan is to evacuate the science team, our wounded man, and our civilian staff. Which means we'll need to create a safe route to the forward deck, then form a secure perimeter around the helipad. Any questions?" Moss briefly glances from one side of the group to the other; he sees only clarity and purpose on the faces standing in front of him. "We have a mission to complete, gentlemen. Let's get to it."

Moving silently as one unit, with the civilians in the rear, Moss leads his fully armed team through the ship's interior. They rapidly advance down the corridor, which leads to the forward deck and the helipad. One crewman helps Randy, their injured man, to keep up; his mangled leg is now bandaged inside a splint. The crushed doors that lead outside to the helicopter pad lay ahead of them. The group maintains their swift pace as they pass by a row of shattered windows. The men's combat boots crunch into the broken glass scattered across the floor as they continue to move forward.

Then Moss spots movement up ahead: shapes at the end of the passageway. It's difficult to make out at first, as the doors at the end of the darkened corridor lay open to the bright sunlight. The intense glare makes it almost impossible to see. Moss raises his hand and signals everyone to halt. He then signals the men to fan out as they form a line across the corridor, establishing an armed shield between themselves and the civilians huddled behind them. Then Moss' blood suddenly runs cold as he sees what is emerging from the glare. They move over the deck of the ship as if they were still in the ocean. As the zombie sharks become fully visible, their ravaged, reanimated bodies are now badly decomposed, with jagged cuts marking where their fins had once been, their dead eyes bleached white, their jaws endlessly snapping. Moss realizes the mission he and his team have taken on will be much more difficult than he anticipated.

The powerful stench emanating from the horde is overwhelming as the zombies glide effortlessly toward Moss and his team. Moss knows the sharks will relentlessly seek a target, and his only chance will be to strike first. He quickly estimates there are perhaps forty, but it's hard to tell as they flow in a mass straight for him. "Make sure they're in range, guys," he orders. Moss takes aim with his Taser, waits until he's certain the weapon's electrodes will hit their target, then pulls the trigger as the rest of the men begin firing. Eight, perhaps, ten sharks are immediately destroyed in the first go. However, the horde isn't affected; it continues to rapidly flow toward them. Moss can see more zombie sharks filling the corridor ahead; they are now rushing in like a river through the doors that lead to the helipad.

Moss quickly holsters his Taser, then whips out a pair of stun batons. "MOVE!" Moss orders, as he marches forward. With a stun baton in each hand, Moss rapidly begins jamming the batons into the sharks now snapping all around him. Rafferty is right beside him, taking out one slimy zombie shark after the other, while Murray and the other nine men fire their Tasers.

The air fills with the crackle of electrical weapons' discharge as the team steadily advances down the corridor. In the flurry of flying electrodes, the sharks leap up, convulse, and fall to the floor in front of them. The team calmly step over the growing pile of de-animated corpses as the veteran mercenaries continue to gain ground. They've almost reached the opening that leads to the helipad when the men begin to hear an unmistakable steady beat coming from outside. "MOVE!" Moss shouts once more. "We gotta go now!" The men begin to run, forcing their way down the rest of the corridor; blasting through the zombie shark horde in a storm of electrical discharges and putrid, splattering fish matter.

* * *

Inside the storage bay, Marsh leans over to nudge a dozing Falcon. "Hey Tom, you hear that?"

Falcon opens his eyes. "What am I supposed to be hearing?"

"Just listen, Tom; I think it's a helicopter."

Falcon stands, then he hears it too. "Do you think it's the Coast Guard?"

"No," answers Marsh, "I know that sound... that's Flip."

"What the hell is a *Flip*?"

Marsh excitedly leaps to his feet. "Flip is the chief pilot. He's been in Manila the past three weeks servicing the ship's helicopter. I know that's him; he must be coming in to land on the helipad."

Falcon calmly walks over to the backpack; he reaches inside, then pulls out the Taser and stun baton.

"What are you doing, Tom? This our chance to get off this ship. They're going to evacuate. That's why he's here; we can escape!"

"Peter, you don't understand" Falcon's tone is cold and determined. "We can't leave until I get that talisman back." Falcon puts the backpack down, then he looks at Marsh. "There will be no stop to this. The horde will just keep growing, no matter how many sharks get destroyed or finally rot away; more will replace them, and more people will die, Peter. Who knows how many, and the only way to end this is if you and I can get that sub launched. I must get that talisman back, Peter. I have no choice, and I can't do it without you, which means you're in this now whether you like it or not."

Marsh looks at his friend, while he listens to the approaching chopper; the sound is a powerful temptation. Marsh knows the helicopter could be his only chance to escape, but as Falcon's words sink in, he realizes he truly has no choice but to follow through with Falcon's plan. "Well then old friend, I guess we'd better get that sub launched. Mr. Moss and his men will be plenty busy up at the bow. This is our perfect opportunity, right?"

"Absolutely," answers Falcon. "Now grab your Taser; we have a mission to complete."

* * *

From the air, Flip catches his first glimpse of *Fearless* as she drifts helplessly a few hundred meters from shore. "Jesus…" Flip whispers as he spots the smashed-out windows of the bridge and a deck crawling with hundreds of sharks. Then, out through the broken doors to the forward deck bursts a full combat contingent with weapons blazing. Flip can see they're surrounded, and that his shipmates are in trouble. From his vantage point inside the helicopter, Flip painfully watches as Ax, Razz, and the rest of his friends fire in all directions, ferociously battling their way to the helipad. *No time for a radio call*, Flip thinks as he flies an un-armed, luxury chopper into a live fire emergency evacuation.

On deck, Alistair Fairchild has yet to see a zombie shark in full motion as he clings desperately to the belt of the crewman in front of him. His heart pounds and sweat stings his eyes, as everything around him swirls in a blur. He keeps his head low as he's pulled forward, doing all he can to avoid tripping over the dead sharks that drop by the dozen in front of him. His sneakers are now soaked with rotten fish flesh; the stench causes him to gag. He briefly glances over at the other civilians that run beside him; their faces are filled with horror as they see what lies in front of them, but Alistair can't bring himself to look. Then a gust of wind hits his face. He looks up to see the chopper approaching, and he realizes he's going to survive this.

Chapter 29

Falcon throws open the hatchway and fires his Taser at close range, aiming it directly into a pack of rabidly snapping jaws. The electrodes strike and instantly destroy multiple targets. "It works great!' Falcon shouts. "Look at that!" He glances back at a startled Marsh. "Peter! Come on, just follow me!" Marsh holds his Taser at the ready, but Falcon is doing the job for both of them as he jams the baton into zombie sharks with one hand, while firing the Taser with the other. "Quick!" Falcon shouts at Marsh. "Up the ladder with you!" Marsh quickly climbs up to the hydraulic lift's controls, while Falcon covers him from below.

"What do I do now?' Marsh shouts down to Falcon. "There're so many of them!"

"Your fucking weapon!" Falcon bellows without looking up. "That fucking thing in your hand! Use it!"

"Oh, right…"

Marsh draws his Taser and fires. He's instantly impressed by the effectiveness of the stun gun, and surprised by the personal satisfaction he suddenly feels, as he obliterates several reanimated sharks with each shot. Falcon has left Marsh to clear his own path to the mini-sub. As he reaches the sub's hatch, he opens it, then shouts once more up to Marsh, "Peter! Here! Catch!" Marsh looks in Falcon's direction to see the stun baton tumbling through the air directly at him. It hits him in the chest. Marsh fumbles a bit, but manages to grab hold of it before it drops. Marsh then watches as Falcon begins to strap himself into the sub. He suddenly realizes he's now on his own, and the chilling reality of what he's actually doing terrifies him.

The success of their *mission* now rests completely on his shoulders; Marsh must somehow hold the sharks at bay, while he simultaneously launches the mini-sub. Then he'll have to make it back to the hatchway without Falcon's help. Severe anxiety rapidly grows inside Peter Marsh as he attempts to fight off the zombie sharks that are now closing in all around him. A large shape catches his attention, Marsh glances away from the sub to see a four-meter-long, zombie great white shark moving rapidly toward him. And for a split second, he's mesmerized; the great white is one of his personal favorites. Then the fact that this one is a zombie trying to kill him clicks in.

The reanimated great white shark is less than two meters away when Marsh finally fires his Taser. As the electrodes strike the killer shark, the high-voltage charge sends the creature into instant convulsions. Marsh is suddenly filled with a powerful surge of confidence as the massive shark drops to the deck. "Wow!" Marsh shouts. "That was amazing!"

* * *

Moss catches brief glimpses of the shimmering, metallic grey, Bell 429 descending toward the helipad as he jams his stun batons into one zombie shark after the other. His team, with civilians in tow, have made it through the doorway to the forward deck; they are now out in the open. "Clear the pad!" Moss shouts. His crew ready their Herstal SLP tactical shotguns loaded with the XREP cartridges. The helipad is seething with a mass of rotted shark flesh; in its current state, it will be impossible to land on. Multiple rounds of shotgun blasts fill the air; the XREP cartridges work perfectly, but the putrid remains of long-dead sharks now blanket the helipad.

Time to improvise... Moss thinks. As the team surmounts the helipad, the armed crewmen fan out to form a secure perimeter with the civilians inside. While Moss turns inward, he spots Alistair. "Get these sharks out of here! You guys! Now! Clear this deck!" Alistair reaches down to grab the tail of a dead gray shark; its rough hide cuts into his skin as he drags the heavy corpse to one side. The ship's civilian staff immediately go to work grabbing dead sharks, then dragging them to the edge where *Fearless'* armed crew continue to fire their weapons while the deafening thunder of pump-action shotgun blasts echoes out across the water.

As Flip descends, the sounds of the battle raging beneath him fills the cockpit of his chopper. He tries to filter out the sounds and focus only on his landing, but as the surreal scene beneath him comes into full view, he's suddenly filled with the familiar surge of adrenaline he felt in combat. He figures he'll have just enough room inside the helipad to land safely as long the guys can hold back those sharks. From his vantage point, however, Flip can see there's a lot of them, much more than what the crew can see from the helipad. As Flip briefly scans the waterline of *Fearless*, he spots what must be thousands more in the ocean. He can see countless numbers buzzing madly all around her; the sight momentarily reminds him of an angry hornet's nest, but these aren't hornets, they're deadly sharks. As Flip continues to zero in on his target, he tunes out everything else, and focuses his mind totally on his mission.

* * *

Marsh is now operating the hydraulic crane. As the crane begins to lift the sub from its platform, it's clear to him the wave of sharks that washed over the length of the ship must have hit it. As the cable tightens, the sub begins sliding. Marsh can see it's way off center. The mini-sub has been turned almost one hundred eighty degrees from its normal position. Marsh wonders if it's ok. Is the sub even going to be operational once it's in the water? He raises the sub up from the platform, then begins to swing the crane's lift arm out and away from the ship, when he suddenly sees more zombie sharks coming at him.

His hands leave the crane's controls as he turns to fire. The sub is swaying back and forth as the hydraulic lift arm continues to move on its own. Meanwhile Falcon is inside; he's trying to get the sub's systems up and running, but he can do nothing as he looks back to see Marsh firing at the sharks. The lift arm, unmanned, slowly rumbles as it swings the sub out over the water. Marsh starts to panic as even more sharks come at him, far more than before. He briefly turns to see the sub dangling out over the water. He hurriedly grabs for the lever that would slowly begin to extend the cable, and allow the mini-sub to lower down to the sea, but in his haste, Marsh hits the cable's emergency release by mistake. The cable suddenly lets go, and Marsh watches in horror as the mini-sub free falls fifty feet into the water.

* * *

On the helipad, Moss now feels confident they have enough open space for a landing, knowing that Flip could probably make due with even less. He looks up to see the strobe-like effect of the spinning blades slicing through the sunlight as the prop wash hits him. And for a split-second Moss is back in Afghanistan, watching an approaching Black Hawk that will extract him and his team to safety. But this chopper isn't here for him; he won't be leaving his ship.

Flip begins his landing sequence, initiating his final descent to the helipad; *just like a bee landing on a flower...* the same thought passes through his head before each and every touchdown. It's what his primary instructor used to say, and ever since hearing it, the phrase has become his personal good luck charm. Flip glances down at the computerized instruments displayed by the Bell's BasiX-Pro avionics screens; he spots his SASR patch pinned to the instrument panel: *Those Who Dare Win...* The chopper is now only a few meters above the deck. Flip continues his descent, and never stops flying until he feels the rails softly bump the surface, then he throttles back.

He sees Moss, Flip pulls his headset off as Moss opens the cockpit door. "Can you take all these people?"

It's called *full gross load*, and it's the maximum takeoff weight every aircraft, whether fixed wing or rotorcraft, has been certified with. A mathematical formula that calculates the weight of the aircraft when it's completely empty against everything it's carrying, such as fuel, passengers, and baggage, along with the amount of horsepower needed to take off and fly.

Of course the maximum horsepower is fixed. In the case of the Bell, she's powered by twin Pratt & Whitney turboshaft engines, each rated at 1,100 shp. Then there's the dry weight of the aircraft itself, which is also fixed. The one variable that's always in question, which must be calculated carefully against the parts of the equation that don't change, is the ratio of fuel, passengers, and baggage. Of course any pilot who swears he's never flown *over gross* is lying through his teeth. Flying over gross was the standard during Flip's military days, but it's hard on the aircraft, not to mention dangerous. In his current life as a civilian pilot, he has avoided the practice religiously. Flip confidently looks at Moss. "Yeah, I can do it."

. . .

From his elevated position standing at the control panel of the hydraulic crane, Marsh watches in horror as the mini-sub hits the water, splashing in like an Apollo capsule on reentry. "No no no no!" Peter screams as he desperately searches the sea below, hoping for a glimpse of his friend, but there is none. Marsh can't see any sign of Falcon as the mini-sub briefly bobs on the surface, then slowly sinks. "What have I done?' Marsh cries. "God no, please no!" Marsh is reeling from his mistake, grieving for his friend he's certain he's just killed, when he makes another one; he forgets where he is, and the danger he's in.

The first zombie shark to attack him is only a smallish gray reef shark, its fierce little jaws gnawing into Marsh's lower calf muscle hardly register. In his traumatized state, he doesn't even feel the second shark grab his left arm, even though it's much bigger, a zombie white tip nearly three meters in length. It's also got his stun-baton; the strap hanging from his left arm is hopelessly shredded as the shark tears through it and the baton falls to the deck.

Marsh suddenly senses the stabbing pain, but it's still not as great as the suffering he feels over killing his friend. Suspended in a haze of extreme emotional shock, Peter Marsh looks at the zombie white tip gnashing into his flesh, and as strange as it seems, his last coherent thought is purely scientific; pondering the sensation, the mechanics of the shark's anatomy, the fact that the zombie shark's jaws still function so well long after life has left its body. As the hundreds of razor-sharp teeth lining the white tip's jaws slice into his arm, Marsh suddenly remembers the Taser in his right hand. Pointing it at the shark, he pulls the trigger, but the weapon only emits a low buzz, indicating it's out of charge.

Chapter 30

As the mini-sub slowly sinks, Falcon's unconscious body lies slumped to one side, still strapped into his seat. His head is bleeding, and the impact has left the sub severely damaged; it's now sinking out of control to the reef below. Outside, the zombie horde schools relentlessly. There are so many of them now; if Falcon were conscious, he would hardly see water. The ravaged, decomposed corpses of the reanimated sharks flow past the acrylic viewing port of the sub in an endless circle of reanimated death.

The sub shudders as the zombie sharks, drawn by Falcon's own life force, begin to attack, as if in a jealous rage, envious of a body that is still in possession of life. They strike at the sub viciously, pounding their own rotting bodies against the structure, trying to rip it open, so they can tear apart the man inside. The damaged seal around the escape hatch is the first to give way as a high-pressure spray of seawater suddenly erupts inside the sub's cabin. The water hits Falcon, and as it continues to spray against his face and body, he gradually regains consciousness.

Pale blue light from the sun filtering down through the sea fills the sub's interior. Falcon slowly wipes the stinging saltwater from his eyes, then looks down at his hands. His vision is still fuzzy, but he can make out the blood. The throbbing pain in his head must be the source, he reasons, as he rubs his bloody hands across his jeans. The sub suddenly lurches; Falcon looks out of the giant acrylic viewing dome in front of him. The sea on the other side of the transparent shell is packed full of grotesquely decomposed zombie sharks that are all trying to kill him. "Looks like the old shaman was right," Falcon says out loud to no one but himself. "This is one hell of a path I'm on."

As he regains greater coherence, Falcon begins to assess the mini-sub's systems. The sub's electric engine is not working, radio communications are not working, the depth meter and cabin atmosphere gauges are not working, the cabin lights aren't working either, nor the exterior lights. The sub is dead in the water, and Falcon knows he would be too except for one thing; he has a job to do.

* * *

On deck, Moss and Rafferty quickly help their civilian staff and the two remaining members of the science team climb into the chopper. Randy, his mangled right leg held in a splint, is the last to board, taking the empty copilot's seat up front next to Flip. The chopper was designed for eight; it's now carrying twelve. Moss slides the passenger door closed, then immediately turns to rejoin the fight. He knows they must keep the helipad clear as Flip spools up the rotors and throttles the twin turbine engines up to full power. With the engines now running at maximum output, the Bell sluggishly lumbers into the air. She rises almost imperceptibly at first, but then gradually builds momentum as Flip patiently waits for the chopper to develop enough lift to fly. Moss doesn't look back as he and the rest of his crew continue to fight off the fast-converging horde of zombie sharks. He can tell by the sound that Flip has his bird in the air.

As the crippled sub descends into darkness, it begins to slowly spin, rotating in a drunken, uneven sort of way, which gives Falcon brief views of the outside. At one point he catches sight of *Fearless*, with the unmistakable outline of her hull enveloped in the horde as she drifts dangerously close to a coral ledge. Another slow turn... the sub sinks deeper, and Falcon observes that the zombie sharks appear to be thinning out. Which tells him the horde is mostly clustered at the surface near *Fearless*.

Then a loud crunch ripples through the mini-sub, resulting in a hard jerk that throws Falcon against the safety harness holding him into his seat. The initial impact is followed closely by the loud scraping sounds of metal against rock. Falcon looks out through the viewing dome and sees that the sub has hit bottom. From what he can surmise, she appears to be tenuously perched on the side of a coral ledge, but not for long, as the sub begins sliding further into the depths.

CRACK! The shark's impact has caught Falcon off guard, but her appearance startles him back to full coherence. He quickly glances down at his feet and grabs for a duffle bag lying on the floor. He'd left it inside the sub the night he successfully slipped out of his cabin to steal its keys, and by chance, to pilfer Alistair's stun baton. As he lifts the bag, the sub is suddenly struck again, knocking it from his hands as he's thrown once more against his safety harness. The sub's stainless steel outer frame continues to slide down over the coral, sending grinding shrieks of scraping, tearing metal into Falcon's ears as he searches the water outside. Then he catches a brief glimpse as she quickly darts in front of the viewing dome. Falcon is suddenly energized with confidence as he recognizes the female tiger shark. His mission is now back on track, as he realizes he is exactly where he is supposed to be.

From inside the helicopter, Alistair Fairchild is in a state of shock. He watches silently out the window as the Bell 429 slowly rises from the deck. Rapid weapons fire blasts from the pump-action SLPs coupled with sporadic submachine gun fire; the percussion fills the chopper's passenger cabin. This, along with the high-pitched whine of the turbine engines running for all they're worth, forms a chaotic combination that signals overwhelming danger, freaking out everyone inside except Randy and Flip. Alistair is crammed into the rear corner of the compartment. The cabin is packed with passengers all sitting on top of each other. One of the kitchen staff is sitting on the floor in front of Alistair, he leans against Alistair's legs as if they were the back of a seat. The rising stench of the rotted shark flesh splattered all over the passengers, combined with human sweat, quickly overwhelms the fragrance of fine leather and new carpet.

Sitting partially on top of Alistair is his lab partner Brian, as he also cranes to see outside, he holds his phone up to the glass. "Holy shit!" Brian shouts as the full scope of the devastation below becomes visible. As the helicopter gains altitude, the zombie shark-covered deck of the three-hundred-and-eighteen-foot vessel unfolds beneath them. Alistair can't see any way out for Moss and his men; from his viewpoint, the situation looks hopeless. He and Brian can see the circle of hardened mercenaries standing on the helipad shoulder to shoulder, fiercely fighting off what looks like an overwhelming horde. The helipad now stands alone; a speck of an island in a raging sea of death.

Alistair is filled with sadness that Dr. Marsh himself is not with them. The horrific scene becomes too overwhelming for the young grad student; he turns away and begins to cry. Brian is still straining to see, however; he pushes the weeping Alistair aside as he leans in for a better view. That's when he notices the mini-sub is missing. He's not sure why, but he's certain Dr. Marsh and Dr. Falcon have something to do with it.

Chapter 31

The wrecked, three-man mini-sub finally comes to rest after sliding to the bottom of a long, sloping coral ledge. The loud grinding and shrill scraping sounds have ceased, and the zombie sharks are no longer visible outside the viewing dome. Except for the soft trickle of seawater, Falcon now finds himself in near total silence. Through the viewing dome, he can see a vast landscape of coral mounds. The scientist inside Falcon can't help but take note that the environment is totally devoid of fish life. This reef is clearly healthy, Falcon observes, with an extensive array of colorful hard and soft corals; it should be bustling with an equally large variety of tropical reef fish, but the place is a ghost town.

Falcon releases his harness and looks down at his feet; they're wet, resting in what looks like ten centimeters of fast-rising water. "Well then," says Falcon, "that's a positive development…" Falcon then opens the duffle bag. Inside are a set of dive fins, a weight belt, a dive mask, and a small SCUBA tank mounted with a regulator. As Falcon bends down to put on his fins, he is suddenly stopped by the throbbing pain in his head. He reaches up and feels the sticky blood now matted into his hair. Then he looks back down at the rising water now nearly up to his knees. "Almost there…"

* * *

With the chopper gone, Moss feels a sense of relief that the evacuation was successful, but he also recognizes the rapidly deteriorating situation for his men and himself. With Dr. Falcon's zombie shark horde now rapidly closing in on them, Moss knows that if he ever sees the guy again, he'll kill him. Moss has used up his stun batons along with the rest of the men. Most all of the XREP cartridges have been fired as well, and the Tasers are finished. Moss has now reverted back to his MP5, along with most of his team. They've formed a tight circle facing outward. Moss briefly turns back toward the doors they came through; the deck is a solid mass of zombie sharks. It's not looking good. He glances at Rafferty, who is standing right next to him.

"We gotta get out of here now!" Moss shouts

"That's for damn sure!" Razz answers,

Then Moss looks Razz in the eye. "Time to improvise."

Razz looks back at Moss. "Shit…"

* * *

With the rapidly rising seawater now nearly up to his neck, Falcon painfully pulls on his dive mask, then shoves the regulator into his mouth, and dips down below the surface. Breathing through the regulator, He reaches down and grabs the handle to the escape hatch. Falcon then braces himself against the back of the rear seat and turns the handle. The hatch swings open as the remaining air inside the mini-sub floods out in a cloud of bubbles. Falcon pulls himself free of the sub, slipping easily through the small hatch, and out into the open sea.

The first thing Falcon hears are rapid, sporadic popping sounds. He's certain it's gunfire coming from the ship above him. He then looks in all directions, and sees no sign of the tiger shark. He begins swimming toward a large coral mound just a few meters away, careful to conserve his air. Falcon looks back at the sub; it's badly crushed and mangled. He's amazed it held together at all; a testament to the expertise of its construction, he surmises.

He looks up to see the horde raging on the surface, thousands of sharks silhouetted against a sunlit sky. The churning chaos is concentrated around the huge dark outline of *Fearless* looming above him. They're mostly right against her hull, circling madly, as they froth the sea white in a storm of pure death. The ship is about to strike the reef, but Falcon knows he can do nothing about it. Then a flash of movement catches his attention; he knows it's her. As he reaches the coral mound, he sees an opening, a crevice near its base. Falcon pulls himself inside and waits.

* * *

For Moss and his team aboard *Fearless*, the intense flurry of machine gun fire is deafening, as the onslaught of zombie sharks continues to build. The more reanimated corpses Moss and his crew manage to pile-up, the more the horde keeps expanding, as the men realize they're now trapped on the helipad, cut off from escape. The crew of *Fearless* struggle to maintain the ground around them. With each advance they make, waves of raging rotting shark corpses flood in to fill the void and drive them back. The zombies' wildly snapping jaws draw ever closer as the team fights to maintain their meager hold on the helipad. Moss looks again at Rafferty; he signals Razz with a quick nod as he pulls a grenade from his vest. "Shit…" Rafferty says once more as Moss pulls the pin. "GRENADE!" Rafferty shouts, then Moss repeats the warning as he throws the live grenade into the heaviest part of the horde on top of the hatches to the tender bay.

The men hear the word *grenade*, and the seasoned mercenaries all instinctively drop to the deck. They leap back toward the center of the helipad as the armed explosive flies over their heads. Moss waits until he sees that the grenade will strike his target before ducking down himself. The resulting explosion sends pieces of rotted shark meat in all directions as a reeking shower of liquefied matter sprays across the team lying face down on the helipad. The doors to the tender bay instantly collapse, as a river of zombie sharks, destroyed zombie sharks, and pieces of zombie sharks flood inside. Their slimy bodies quickly fill the compartment below.

In the aftermath, Moss is the first to jump back to his feet, but as he does, the ship begins listing to one side as *Fearless* grounds on the reef beneath her. Moss is knocked back down to the deck as the rest of his men attempt to hold on, while a horrible groan fills the air as her steel hull crumples against the rocks below.

* * *

Falcon peers out through the narrow opening in the coral mound. He can still hear the muffled popping sounds of automatic weapons fire coming from above. Then it stops momentarily, and he hears an explosion. *Shit...* Falcon thinks, just as a dark shape passes in front of his field of view. He leans forward to look, just as her massive jaws armed with rows of sharp white teeth flash in front of his face. He pushes himself back as the zombie tiger shark fights to get into the opening. She's snapping madly, forcing herself deeper into the crevice, sending up a cloud of debris as fragments of coral rain down. Her jaws are only inches from Falcon's face when he sees it: the talisman.

As the zombie tiger shark continues to attack, a low rumbling sensation ripples through the water, and Falcon feels trembling in the rocks around him; he knows what the source is—*Fearless has struck the reef...*

Falcon studiously scans the zombie shark's snapping jaws as they plunge repeatedly into the narrow opening in front of his face. The zombie tiger shark's attack is beginning to break away layers of coral, as her jaws dig deeper. With each gaping assault, Falcon can see the talisman wedged inside; it's right there in front of him. He watches, and waits for just the right moment, then goes for it. Falcon jams his arm into her mouth just as her lower jaw briefly catches on the rock-hard edge of the opening.

He thrusts his right hand inside the tiger shark's huge jaws and attempts to grab the talisman. Falcon briefly feels the talisman brush across his fingertips just as the zombie shark's jaws break free of the coral and snap shut. He is instantly in agony as the regulator slips from his mouth and Falcon cries out uncontrollably. His right wrist is now trapped, clinched tightly between her jaws as she begins to violently shake herself free. The tiger shark thrashes her head rapidly back and forth; Falcon feels the horrible sensation of his hand being torn from his body as he's bashed against the coral. The zombie tiger shark's gnashing jaws crush the bones of his right wrist, as they tear through his flesh, then bone, then finally rip free.

* * *

As *Fearless* grounds onto the coral ledge, she lists to port, as the surf begins to batter her starboard side. In the aftermath of the explosion, Moss and his team are back on their feet, but they look on in disgust as the void created by the explosion quickly disappears. The horde is flowing onto the deck once more, as if the horde was regenerating itself automatically. Then Moss hears a scream, he sees Cal; a zombie shark has him by the leg, Moss begins firing off rounds from his MP5, as the reanimated dead shark drags Cal toward the horde. Then Rafferty lets loose with his P90, he watches as the rounds rip through rotted flesh, allowing Cal to break free from the shark's grip. Even though he's bleeding badly, Cal gets back on his feet and returns to the battle. He knows he has no choice; it's fight or die.

Then the men hear another painful cry as a large zombie hammerhead lunges at Steve. Its crazed, snapping jaws hit him in the gut, then bite down hard as the hammerhead begins to thrash violently. Cal and Murray pump bullets into its rotting corpse, but the zombie hammerhead's teeth only plunge deeper into Steve's torso as it shakes its head. Cal, and the rest of the team, are fighting desperately to save their friend, but then Cal's MP5 fires off its last three rounds. Moss too is firing at the shark when his MP5 runs dry; with their guns empty, the crewmen are filled with furious anger as Steve is dragged into the horde.

Moss tosses the empty gun to the deck, reaches up behind his head and quickly draws the twin Kukri blades from their sheaths strapped to his back. His hands tightly gripping their long, leather-wrapped handles, Moss now holds a blade in each hand, and with powerful swings, begins furiously slicing into the zombie sharks. He tries to reach Steve but it's too late, the men gasp uncontrollably as their friend is torn apart in front of them. "We've gotta get back inside!" Moss shouts as the crew of *Fearless* quickly pool their remaining clips, reload, and regroup.

* * *

Falcon's own blood clouds the water around his battered body as the zombie tiger shark breaks free, taking his right hand with her. Desperately in need of air, he feels for the tank. Falcon grabs it, clears the regulator, and takes in a breath as he sees the tattered remains of his right arm; two jagged bones poke out from his shredded flesh just as she comes at him again. Her jaws are open once more, but now with Falcon's severed right hand inside them. She plunges her head into the crevice, causing the coral to crumble as the opening expands. Falcon tries to push himself deeper inside but there's nowhere else to go; he's out of room.

With each lunge at the coral, the zombie tiger shark forces her head deeper into the opening. She continues to attack, plunging her head into the crevice again and again until she gets stuck once more; her lower jaw firmly catches the jagged edge of the opening. Falcon sees his chance. He doesn't hesitate; he quickly reaches his left hand inside her gaping jaws. He can see his right hand floating loose inside her mouth. He pushes it out of the way and grabs the talisman.

As his left hand closes around the small statue, he feels an intense shock while a powerful sensation spreads through his body. Gripping the talisman tightly, Falcon pulls his left hand free as the massive zombie tiger shark suddenly becomes de-animated. Her body goes instantly rigid, then slowly falls to the sand outside the crevice. Falcon draws one more breath from the small tank and realizes there won't be another one; it's empty. He spits the regulator from his mouth, as he kicks his way out of the crevice. He leaves behind the now-lifeless body of the tiger shark, as she lies once more on her side, exactly the way he had first discovered her.

Chapter 32

Alex Moss swings a Kukri blade in each hand as he battles the raging storm of zombie sharks that are relentlessly trying to kill him. He aims his blows for the moment the shark's jaws open the widest. He is a man whose mind is consumed with rage, his body nearly burnt out from exhaustion, yet explosive satisfaction drives him on; he is now blind to everything but the mission, and the mission is to stay alive. He refines his technique literally on the fly, as he repeatedly levels his blades to cut horizontally across the shark's gaping jaws. With synchronous timing, Moss finds a single, surgically directed strike will neatly divide the upper from the lower mandible, rendering the target inoperable. He doesn't know how many he's taken out, maybe a hundred, maybe more. It's effective, it's medieval, and also extremely tiring; he wishes the Tasers still worked. The muscles in his arms scream as the pile of de-animated dismembered corpses steadily grows.

Losing Steve, seeing another member of his crew die, has sent the anger inside Moss to full throttle. His aching body is now covered in emulsified, decomposed shark flesh. The stench is unbearable, yet there is no end to this hell he and his team have found themselves trapped inside. As the crew of *Fearless* fight on, a relentless flood of zombie sharks flow in from all directions as one by one the men's ammunition runs out. Moss briefly glances to his right as Rafferty's MP90 fires its final rounds. In desperation, Razz drops his empty weapon, then draws a large field knife just as another zombie lunges at him. Inflamed by pure rage, Razz tackles the zombie shark with his bare hands. He throws the eight-foot long shark to the deck, then leaps on top of it, and begins plunging his knife repeatedly into its gills.

A blizzard of wildly snapping jaws surround the crew of *Fearless*. The continuously expanding horde steadily closes in, and the meager patch of deck the men now defend grows ever smaller. Moss and his team fight on with anything they can get their hands on. Moss knows his arms are about to give out; he's facing a battle he can't win, and he's accepted it. But Alex Moss continues to fight, and he will fight for as long as his body will allow him, as the sea around *Fearless* once more disgorges the horde, sending thousands more zombie sharks spilling onto the deck in front of him.

In the insanity of this moment, Moss' mind is spinning; he is still trying to improvise, still searching for a solution, but there isn't one... *How can it end like this?* In an instant, a million thoughts flash through his mind: friends, duty, commitment, his resolve in making the right choices, but also what he'll leave unresolved; the relationships he let pass by... *Trish.* Her face briefly flashes through his head, as he's filled with regret over the family he'll never have. But most of all, the biggest regret, the shame, the unforgivable act of leading his men to their deaths.

Swallowed inside the eye of a cyclone of death, Moss turns to see Razz plunging his knife into another zombie shark, just as two more attack; Moss is in range, but his blades can only reach one of them. "Razz!" Moss shouts as a blade sinks into reanimated flesh, and to his amazement, both sharks suddenly drop to the deck. A stunned Moss quickly looks around; the entire horde has suddenly stopped moving. The exhausted crew of *Fearless* watch in disbelief as hundreds of now de-animated zombie sharks simultaneously fall to the deck in a heap. Moss looks back at his friend; Rafferty is still stabbing his knife into a dead shark, unaware that the ordeal is over, while the rest of the crew cautiously scan the deck of their ship in disbelief. They are still ready, their weapons still raised, as Moss, tightly gripping the handles of his Kukri blades, waits to be sure it's truly over.

* * *

Falcon desperately kicks himself free from the coral crevice. His lungs are on fire as he struggles to hold the last puff of air he sucked from the spent dive tank and swim for the surface. Falcon kicks upwards as hard as he can, while all around him, the bodies of thousands of de-animated sharks drift past him on their way back to the bottom of the sea. The violent hurricane that was once a zombie shark horde has died into a gentle rain. Falcon is focused on the surface above, on the sunlight filtering through the sinking, motionless bodies. Then he sees something else, a movement; something is swimming toward him; it's a snake, a beautifully colored sea snake. As Falcon watches the snake dart back and forth, tasting the bodies of the slowly falling sharks, he realizes his lungs aren't burning anymore. The sense of panic he felt is now gone. Then the snake approaches. Falcon reaches out with the one hand he has left, and the snake touches it with its tongue.

Instantly Falcon finds himself once more standing in the back yard of his grandmother's house in Jamaica. A loving warmth washes over him as he looks down to see he once again has two hands. His clothes are clean; he feels strong. He hears the back door to the porch close; it's his grandmother. She strolls quietly across her neatly mowed yard toward him; she is framed by her garden filled with tropical flowers. Falcon smiles as she walks up to him. "Gramma…"

She reaches out and grasps his hands. "Hush now, Thomas, you still have work to do…"

"But Gramma, what do you mean? I don't understand. I have the talisman."

"Yes, but you still have work to do, so go now. It's time for you to go back, Thomas."

"But, can't I stay here with you?" Falcon looks into the loving eyes of his grandmother as she shakes her head. "No, Thomas, not yet…"

Breaking the surface, Falcon gasps for air as waves of searing pain jolt through his body. The sobering desperation of his reality crashes down on him as he sees the shredded stump that was once his right hand. Falcon treads water and tries to orient himself. He spots *Fearless*; the once-magnificent ship is now helplessly grounded. Her towering bow rises up above him; Falcon can see the crew on deck. He begins swimming toward them, but then Moss catches sight of Falcon in the water. "YOU!" Moss bellows. "You son of a bitch! You come near this vessel—I will kill you myself!"

Chapter 33

Falcon's only choice is to swim for shore. As ocean swell lifts his battered body, he weakly kicks with his dive fins, painfully working his way toward land when he hears the sound of a helicopter overhead. As he struggles to find the strength to swim, he briefly looks up at the shining, metallic gray chopper passing overhead, but Thomas Falcon knows that no rescue will be arriving for him.

* * *

On the deck of *Fearless*, the familiar sound of the Bell GlobalRanger grabs the attention of the beleaguered crew. The growing pulse of chopper blades overhead fills each of them with relief, but as they watch the chopper approach, they're also overcome with sadness for the men they lost. As Flip closes in, he too is struck with grief, as well as dread. From altitude, he quickly assesses the ship's condition: She's severely damaged; she's grounded on the reef, and at the angle she's leaning, there's no way for him to land; even launching the lifeboats could be risky... that is, if anyone survived. Then Flip catches sight of Moss and his crewmates waving at him from the deck of *Fearless*, and the veteran military pilot feels his eyes well up with tears as he sees most of his crewmates are still standing. He radios down to Moss, and after a brief exchange, Flip circles the ship once more, then flies off again, heading for the nearest harbor in search of a boat

As Flip disappears down the coast, Moss turns to his crew. "We need to get below to the engine room and find Pete and Sam. We need to gather medical supplies, water, and we have to take care of the bodies. I want them prepared for transport..." Then Moss pauses. His weathered gaze passes over the traumatized faces of the men standing in front of him. They're not just exhausted, they're totally used up and severely battle worn. Several are wounded; they're covered in sweat and reeking of putrefied shark guts, while their heads pound and their ears wring from the constant percussion of gunfire...

Murray steps forward first. "Right, you heard the chief..."

Then Rafferty gets to his feet; he's bleeding from a bite wound he took in his upper arm. "I'll go below and locate Pete."

Then Seth steps forward. "As ship's medic, I'd like to evaluate the wounded before we start moving around too much. That ok with you, Chief?"

Moss looks at Seth. "Absolutely, examine everyone. I'll go find Pete."

"Chief," Seth puts his hand out, barring Moss from walking off. "You first; your leg is bleeding pretty badly there."

* * *

After hours in the sea, the surf pounding the shore spits Falcon out onto a deserted stretch of beach. His mangled body is now so destroyed that he feels as if the reaper arrived, weighed and measured him, yet found his condition unsuitable even for death's consumption. As he struggles to drag himself through the sand, Falcon senses dry land beneath him for what feels like the first time; then he collapses.

The next day, as Falcon lies unconscious in the sand, a small crowd has gathered around him, curious locals all wanting a look at the dead man that washed up on the beach after the shipwreck. Then the police arrive, but as they begin loading the corpse into a body bag, it suddenly moves, spooking the onlookers. Several gasp and leap back, while others turn and run. Then a man wearing the uniform of the Philippine Coast Guard approaches the police. "Is this man dead?"

"We thought so," one of the police officers responds, "but look, he's moving and making sounds."

"Call an ambulance; this man is now in my custody. He is wanted for crimes against the people of the Philippines."

• • •

From his makeshift operations center set up in a hotel near the wreck site of *Fearless*, Moss coordinates the salvage operation. Members of the Foundation's board of directors have flown in to see the damage for themselves. Meanwhile, the initial recovery and cleanup operation has revealed answers, but also created more questions. They'd found Pete and his assistant Sam, down in the engine room still working; they were nursing the last of the ship's generators in order to keep the bilge pumps running.

The discovery of the remains of Dr. Peter Marsh was a blow to the entire crew. Especially Moss, who not only respected his dedication, reliability, and work ethic; he liked the guy. When the ship's missing sub was located destroyed on the bottom, however, it told Moss what Dr. Marsh was doing outside on deck; he was helping Dr. Falcon. Moss knew Falcon held a submersible operator's license, and Marsh did not. It was Moss who told the Philippine authorities how Dr. Falcon figured into the tragedy at the beach resort, an event the country was publicly mourning. Moss also told the Coast Guard where to find him. Dr. Falcon was now recovering in a hospital under guard, and although the urge to question the man himself is overwhelming, Moss is resisting, not only because he's neck deep in work; he knows if he sees the guy, he'll kill him.

Word of the famous research vessel's incredible battle, and subsequent grounding, spread quickly, as sensationalized news media stories of an *unprecedented series of mass shark attacks* flashed around the world. The rooftop phone video shot by the young Australian couple was leaked online and went viral, until it was mysteriously taken down. Tourism to beach resorts has dropped precipitously worldwide, while the cruise line industry is taking an even bigger hit.

Networks in search of cheap ratings, broadcast live panel discussions-turned live shouting matches between supposed *experts*, a mixed bag of talking heads armed with few facts and a wide range of opinions formulated more to titillate an audience than to inform. The public, as usual, is left largely in the dark, as a cacophony of conflicting information muddies the water. Meanwhile, unprepared and unsuspecting shark biologists are trotted out from their tiny, book-filled university offices to explain on live TV why their science has been so totally off-base. How, they are asked, after all these years, how could a half century of concentrated scientific study miss the existence of such a major phenomenon so completely? The evidence is clear: *Who is to blame?*

* * *

A young woman stands at the front desk of Manila's Metropolitan Medical Center. "Yes, I am a relative, I am his sister. May I see him please?" The nurse on duty takes the woman's identification: "Marcella Falcon..." she says, as she records the information inside the woman's UK passport. The nurse then hands Marcela her passport, along with a clipboard to sign. "See the policemen over there," she says, pointing toward two uniformed officers. "Your brother is a prisoner patient. They will have to escort you." After another identification check, some brief questioning, and one more signature, Marcella enters her brother's guarded hospital room.

"Marcy, wow." Falcon forces a smile through his pain and attempts to sit up as his baby sister enters the room.

"Thomas!" Marcella's eyes fill with tears at the sight of her brother's missing right hand. "What is happening?" she sobs, "Why are all of these police here? What is going on?"

Falcon grasps his sister's hand with the only one he now has left. "There's no time to explain all of this, Marcy."

"You better explain it." Marcela's voice is filled with confusion and anger. "This is crazy! You said nothing about being arrested when you called."

"Look, I need you to do something for me..."

"Thomas, what have you done? Tell me what's going on?"

"I did something stupid, and I deserve everything that is happening to me, and I will explain it all to you, but now is not the time, so please..."

Marcy's face shifts from anger back to sadness, "What is it? What do you need me to do?"

"The police have gone through my belongings, things that were recovered from the ship; they have a bag of personal items they will release to you..."

"Yes..." she answers tentatively.

"In the bag is Gramma's charm, her carving. You know it, right?"

"Of course, I remember."

"I want you to take my things back to Jamaica, and please, be very careful with the charm. I need you to put it someplace safe. Promise me, Marcy, please? This is more important than you'll ever know."

"I understand, I'll do it. You don't need to worry."

* * *

Alistair Fairchild is in his hotel room; he's busily texting friends and family back in New Zealand his schedule now that he's booked his flight home. He pauses to pack the last of the items the crew was able to recover from his cabin aboard *Fearless*, when he hears a knock at the door. Alistair squints through the peephole and sees what looks like two Americans in suits. He opens the door. "Mr. Fairchild? May we have a word with you?" Alistair has never seen these men before, but they look important; *rich* and important. The two men introduce themselves cordially; one is tall, with dark hair, while the other man is slightly shorter and blond. "Alistair," the taller of the two begins, "we wanted to meet with you personally. My colleague and I are board members of the Foundation; may we come inside?"

"Yes, of course," Alistair invites them in, then closes the door behind him as the two men walk to the center of his hotel room. "So, um... what can I do for you gentlemen?" Alistair tries not to show his obvious nervousness, but he's never come in direct contact with the Foundation's leadership before.

The man with blond hair looks directly at Alistair. "We're here on official business Alistair, we have a proposal for you, a job offer of sorts."

Alistair isn't sure what the men are offering. "Um, well, what exactly is a *job offer of sorts?*"

"Think of it as an opportunity," the taller man adds. "We have a long-term project in mind."

Then the shorter, blond-haired gentlemen steps back in. "We'll see to it that you are able to complete your doctorate, then we'll sponsor your research. You'll have the best of everything at your disposal; you'll be working directly for us, of course."

The offer sounded too good to be true, but Alistair has personally experienced the level of financial backing the Foundation is capable of; he's already thinking this deal could be his ticket. "So, what will I be doing exactly? What kind of research do you want me to pursue?"

The two men smile subtly as they briefly glance at each other, then the blond one clears his throat. "Well, Alistair, we want you to research sharks, of course."

"Truly?" Alistair is now even more intrigued.

"Absolutely," the taller man adds. "You will be working exclusively with sharks."

Acknowledgements

The sea is my home. At the moment, the proud city of Auckland is visible from our harbor slip at the Orams Marine Village. We spent a year sailing here from the Balearic Islands in the Mediterranean. Most of this book was written while at anchor in the Kingdom of Tonga, but it was begun in Bora Bora, and made ready for publication in New Zealand. For those who claim that writing is purely a solitary activity, I beg to differ. There are a number of incredible friends and family who helped along the way, who inspired me, supported me, and put up with my irritating moments. This is my first novel, and the challenges seemed vast at first, but as the manuscript progressed, the story took on a life of its own. By the time the final chapter reached its conclusion, the whole project was on rails, and the job became incredibly enjoyable. That said, independent publishing can be as frustrating as it is exhilarating.

Eric, you're awesome. We were relaxing on deck that afternoon, drinking beers and taking in Bora Bora's magical beauty while we brainstormed an outline for a treatment. Afterwards, I was so juiced I whipped out the five-thousand-word treatment in a day, and then spent the next three months writing the first draft of the full novel, all of it on my iPad. It would not have happened without your encouragement and enthusiasm.

For Giamma and Carmen, there is no gratitude I can express here that will come close to showing you both what is in my heart. To simply say thank you is nowhere near enough; I love you both. Thanks for being wonderful.

Ivan, thanks for being funny; I needed that more than you know. And thank you for enjoying my cocktail creations; few pleasures in life surpass a perfectly prepared martini. Mink, thanks for reading Moitessier's *The Long Way* during our passage to New Zealand from Tonga. You reminded me of why we were there, why it's great to be sailing oceans instead of sitting on a couch watching football... or even rugby. Andrea, we've sailed a lot of miles together, and if I could, I would attach a note of appreciation to each one of them.

Finally, a special thank you to Patrizia e Alberto. Your stalwart encouragement and kind notes have been greatly appreciated.

From the Author

Crossing an ocean by sailboat has a lot in common with writing a book, both are daunting at first, and they should be. Respect for the sea will get you across, respect for your reader does the same. I hope you've enjoyed reading my novel, *Death Catch*, writing it has been a fantastic experience, a lot of work, and tremendously fun.

Like most of us enthusiastic readers, I'm sure you skimmed past the Acknowledgments page, but I really was in Bora Bora when I came up with the original concept. French Polynesia is a famously inspiring place, I feel incredibly fortunate to have fallen under her spell.

If you're now a fan of Alex Moss, his gun-toting crew mates, and the lovely lady *Fearless*, please leave a review on Amazon and share with your friends on Twitter, Facebook, Linked In or any book clubs you may belong to. Reviews and personal referrals are the best way for self-published authors to get the word out about a new novel. Competing with the big name publishing houses is